TWISTED TALES

2022

TALES OF ADVENTURE

Edited By Wendy Laws

First published in Great Britain in 2022 by:

Young Writers
Remus House
Coltsfoot Drive
Peterborough
PE2 9BF
Telephone: 01733 890066
Website: www.youngwriters.co.uk

Printed and bound in the UK by BookPrintingUK
Website: www.bookprintinguk.com
YB0514B

FOREWORD

Welcome, Reader!

Come into our lair, there's really nothing to
fear. You may have heard bad things about the
villains within these pages, but there's more
to their stories than you might think...

For our latest competition, Twisted Tales, we challenged
secondary school students to write a story in just 100
words that shows us another side to the traditional
storybook villain. We asked them to look beyond the evil
escapades and tell a story that shows a bad guy or girl in
a new light. They were given optional story starters for a
spark of inspiration, and could focus on their motivation,
back story, or even what they get up to in their downtime!

And that's exactly what the authors in this anthology
have done, giving us some unique new insights into
those we usually consider the villain of the piece.
The result is a thrilling and absorbing collection
of stories written in a variety of styles, and it's a
testament to the creativity of these young authors.

Here at Young Writers it's our aim to inspire the
next generation and instill in them a love of creative
writing, and what better way than to see their work
in print? The imagination and skill within these pages
are proof that we might just be achieving that aim!
Congratulations to each of these fantastic authors.

CONTENTS

Lily Blowers (12)	70	Emily Sanders (11)	113
Lilia Rebihi (13)	71	Jacob Haynes	114
Mikaeel Keyaan Hussain (11)	72	Olivia Terrell	115
Feyisola Ogunsaju (12)	73	Lynn Guo (15)	116
Ibrahim Karim Sangarie (11)	74	Maya Valero Teuma (12)	117
Alice Walker (11)	75	Zainab Safeer (12)	118
Hanna Khan	76	Jessica Mallett (14)	119
Maria Binoy (15)	77	Amber Antoine (10)	120
Devan Babbra (13)	78	Vipul Jain	121
Nimarpreet Singh (12)	79	Diala Farmer (17)	122
Olivia Monk (14)	80	Archie Robinson (13)	123
Jasmine-Ann Chambers (13)	81	Maison Steele	124
Andrew Carroll (12)	82	David Swales (12)	125
Adaya Moses	83	Leon Ridey (11)	126
Sophia Dobson (12)	84	Caitlin Banfield (14)	127
Charlie Evans (13)	85	Sydney Edwards (15)	128
Lara Patel (13)	86	Leon Anish (13)	129
Kristen Judd	87	Muhammad Akhtar (13)	130
Dylan Edwards (12)	88	Jamie Peacock (12)	131
Joshua Williams-Davies (12)	89	Katie Mitchell (16)	132
Sienna Fraser (17)	90	Alana Pope (15)	133
Tilly Byatt	91	Eva Taylor-Williams (13)	134
Salina Mobeen (12)	92	Oscar Meek	135
Kira Riley (11)	93	Mariyam Ali (13)	136
Lucky Gu	94	Libby Goode (13)	137
Aoife Walsh (12)	95	Nadine Pedrick (14)	138
Lauren Mitchell (14)	96	Amelie Putt (12)	139
Kyla Barney	97	Lucy Harris (17)	140
Maisy Clint (11)	98	Lucia Baker (14)	141
Ruqayyah Aziz (14)	99	Caroline Newton (12)	142
Alice Faulkner (13)	100	Chulu Feni (14)	143
Malaika Kitheka (12)	101	Harley Crossman (13)	144
Zahir Alam (12)	102	Isobel Heald (13)	145
Ellie-Jayne Scott	103	Ruby Pike	146
Eloise Moody	104	Kamsana Kalaivasan (15)	147
Lauren Neighbour (16)	105	Leonie Hanan (14)	148
Ele Pike (16)	106	Jessica Edgar (12)	149
Brandon Gadsby-Cooper (13)	107	Garry Cunningham (17)	150
Jess Porter (13)	108	Faye Perry (12)	151
Nahla Salim (13)	109	Christopher McComish (13)	152
Gurman Kaur (13)	110	Ella Shani	153
Aavni Rao (12)	111	Mariama Nyallay (14)	154
Tasnim Sheikh (13)	112	Roxana Anderson-Cristea (12)	155

Aksa Ahmed (16)	156	Esther Woods (12)	199
Millie Graves (13)	157	Emily Edgar (12)	200
Lucy Daw (14)	158	Emma Boyce (12)	201
Alyssa Cupid (15)	159	Kayla Enamu (12)	202
Nana-Oye Appiah (16)	160	Eleanor Restell (11)	203
Toni Agbede (17)	161	Ryan Al-Turk (15)	204
Kiera Crouch (13)	162	Haleema Zeeshan (11)	205
Piranavi Chandrasekaran (13)	163	Oliver Campbell	206
Sahar Ahmed	164	Faith Carter (14)	207
Savanna Puk (12)	165	Finlie Hynd (14)	208
Freya Wright (11)	166	Jaiden White (16)	209
Lydia Alford (12)	167	Maisie Leigh (11)	210
Maria Magalhaes McKown (13)	168	Caitlin Clay (11)	211
Ilana Taylor (15)	169	Connie Edina Gray (14)	212
Porshad Anooshah	170	Amelia Swingewood (11)	213
Harry Harper (11)	171	James Thomas	214
Max Piercy (13)	172	Jacob Syms (13)	215
Nyra Hernandez	173	Dennis Christopher (14)	216
Connie Allen (11)	174	Antos Thomas (12)	217
Maaria Najeeb (13)	175	Finley Mackay (11)	218
Rital Badewi (12)	176	Chloe Bromley (13)	219
Sebastian Schönrock (13)	177	Joe Nsengimana (13)	220
Mishel Mir (13)	178	Isla McCallion (11)	221
Menaal Khan	179	Edwin Jaimon	222
Isabelle Anderson (12)	180	Benjy Harris	223
Zahara Ali (11)	181	Liliana Janovicova (11)	224
Edith Parker-Gerrity (14)	182	Kyla Raschke (13)	225
Bernadette Trimmings (13)	183	Izza Andlib (12)	226
Seren Mai Williams (13)	184		
Lacey Jane Scott (11)	185		
Muhammed Safyan Iqbal (12)	186		
Ronaldo Da Costa	187		
Marta Beirao (11)	188		
Laila Sherwen (12)	189		
Zahra Master (12)	190		
Bella Ward (11)	191		
Millie McEvoy (13)	192		
Zakariyah Raja (12)	193		
Caitlin Tabb (14)	194		
Lucie Edgar (11)	195		
Erin Ghaley (12)	196		
Lillian May Pedley (13)	197		
Claudia Mirembe	198		

THE
STORIES

THAT WAS WHEN HE REALISED

"Raven!" Lyrix yelled. Starktus was getting closer. Lyrix's breath lessened. His bone-cold fist gripped her arm. The air went numb. Starktus gripped harder. Lyrix screamed. Her whole body writhed.

"Lyrix!" Raven screamed. He glared at Starktus. "What have you done?"

Starktus smiled. Raven wanted to smack him. "You know," he whispered, "I didn't cause this."

"No," Raven argued. "Tyrell never caused this."

"I never said Tyrell," Starkus said, still smiling, "but other than Tyrell, who has access to the courtyard?"

"I know it's you!" Raven screamed. That was when it hit him. An icy fist gripped his shoulder. "Lyrix..."

Jeyamonika Ponraj (13)

ONE LAST DRINK

Ding-dong. Here she is. "Olivia, come on in!"
"Thanks, Alice."
"Would you like a drink?"
"Oh no, thank you."
Seriously? "Oh, come on."
"Oh alright."
I went over to the bar and prepared our drinks, adding something extra to Olivia's.
"Here you go."
"It's very pink."
It would be more fitting if it was green. "I know, it's strawberry."
She took a sip of her drink. "Wow this is very-" She abruptly stopped and started choking.
"I'm sorry, Olivia, but I couldn't let you tell anyone about my involvement in Sam's murder."
"Alice I..."
She fell to the floor.

Grace Vaughan (13)

LIFE AND DEATH ARE TWO SIDES OF THE SKY

Rainfall seeped through the rainforest canopy, soaking us three. Death knelt beside a tree. Life approached me; I was off duty: the rain clouds covered the sun, the moon absent.

"Equino, have you seen Death? Haven't since Midnight."

"Over there. Seems busy."

"Death? What are you doing?" He was slashing his scythe at a branch.

"This monkey. She fell from the tree. Legs broken. Won't live. Wanted her favourite berry before that!" Some were in his hands.

"How sweet!"

"Not the only thing sweet; the fruit's also. After all..." he lent some, "...you made it, and it reflects you *perfectly*."

Navvya Makwana (13)

DEATH AND DESIRE

Smeared in blood, I returned with it. Carelessly tossing the corpse, another trophy for my collection. Rue pranced forward with a devilish smile.

"My love! Back so quick?"

"You know commoners are sport; easy, thrilling."

"Disgustingly beautiful! His Majesty shall welcome you surely."

"Work for that snobby snake? Never. Your obsession with him grows every day, it seems - it gives the impression you'd even worship his 'highness' like the rest.

"Come now! You shan't make silly jokes like that."

"But it's the truth... Princess."

I uncovered the royal emblem branded onto her arm.

A scream, silenced by a single shot.

Birluv Singh (11)

THE DARKEST NIGHT IN PENNSYLVANIAN HISTORY

A monstrous solitary figure was in an unusual area in Pennsylvania. He inquisitively glared as President Noah Williams' lustrous Cadillac parked outside City Centre Hospital. He was prepared for the revenge he'd waited for! July 4th, 1939, Darkseid anticipated keeping the President captive. Firstly, he needed an FBI uniform. Sneakily, Darkseid snuck behind the FBI agent, thrashed him several times before dropping unconsciously on the ground. He bolted to the President's office and struck missiles at City Centre Hospital. Colossus Barnes, hero of Pennsylvania was resting on his deathbed, instantly missiles detonated the hospital and shattered it into pieces.

Faizan Shahbaz (14)

WHO IS THE FAIREST OF THEM ALL?

"Mirror, mirror on the wall, who is the fairest of them all?" The mirror spoke two clear words, before changing into a spiral of hypnosis.

"Not yet."

The Evil Queen twitched, trying to escape its wrath.

"Only one thing is stopping you, Snow White," the 'mirror' said. "Go on, become the fairest. Kill her."

She twitched before hesitantly grabbing the apple. "Yes, Master."

"Mirror, mirror on the wall, who is the fairest of them all?" she shyly spoke.

"That... would be me." The mirror chuckled. "I win." Laughter was heard, she dropped to the floor with a bang. "You... lose."

Ricky Brown (13)

NOT MY FAULT

"Look, it's not my fault, it's not my fault I'm Death. I do it 'cause I don't have a choice. If I don't do it I die - again. He makes me do it."
"Who's 'he'?"
"Satan, a right div but y'know we all have to make sacrifices."
"So you've killed millions of people? How could you?"
"I told you, not my fault, anyway if I didn't do it he'd kill me and get some other soul to take on the burden."
"I can't believe you, know what? I'm gonna expose you."
Swish.
"That's why I don't do interviews."

Lion Still

TREVOR FIGHTS BACK

For centuries mutated goats have craved troll flesh. They seek to cross over our territory, over the deathly bridge, terrorising our 'trollings'. Little do they know, we Norwegians are about to execute a master plan.
"Baaaaah!" The very sound shakes the ground, there are just three murderous goats travelling today. Our bomb is in position. *Kabooooom!* Twelve legs and three decapitated heads fly through the sunset. Red rain descends!
Centuries in the waiting, we finally are victorious. Humans have misunderstood us since 1841! Now you know the 'real' tale and have met the 'real' villains, the 'three billy goats'.

Dilara Guzel (14)

THE WOLF'S VERDICT

"I did it to survive! You *must* believe me," I pleaded. "I would *never* eat a human outside those circumstances!"

"What circumstances permit you to *eat* a child?" the king exclaimed angrily. I let out a frustrated growl. Things were not working in my favour.

"I regret my actions, your Majesty! But I was starving - I hadn't eaten in *weeks!* I *hate* killing. I'd never kill for pleasure!"

"That is no excuse for murder, wolf. Your punishment..." he paused, "is banishment to the Wild Lands."

I howled. The *Wild Lands!* I didn't deserve this!

Talitha Smart (14)

HÚLÍJĪNG

Mother had long told me tales of those heinous creatures - humans.
I met one of them, when I wandered past the jade border. GaHei, that was his name. He was benevolent, different from Mother's stories. He made the sky lit up with powder. "*Huo yao*," he tells me. *Boom!* How it flared and illuminated the night!
Boom! The same sound I heard that winter morning. My village, burned and bombed. My people, darted, disfigured and dismantled for 'scientific purposes'. GaHei told them... the humans.
Thenceforth, I spend my days hunting them. Not the women. Their husbands certainly tasted much better.

Neera Cheung (16)

CAPTAIN HOOK'S REVENGE

"It's been years, Cap'n!" Smee wails, "we're all to starve: all for one too spritely to grow up. I ask you, where be his power? What's in it for us if he dies?"

"*When* he dies, Mr Smee, When! Of all the yesteryears and tomorrows come, aren't I due revenge?" Hook spits. "It's no petty crime - his parents ruined me! Help me! Face the fairy-child and the crocodile who's possessed by Pan, for his son. Brave Pan..." Captain Hook paces around angrily, "In Shakespeare's words, the name be well deserv-ed. Now, let's get revenge on the lost and found boy."

Becky Turner (15)

WITCH TO WHAT?

I wasn't weak but feared! From a ruthless and dreaded witch to what? Wait till I get my revenge on Oz. Pigtails and her little dog cannot possess my rightful victory. Daydreaming through perpetual darkness, lit a minuscule spark that soon engulfed me with luminosity. Gingerly, I steaded myself. Glaring around the pillars of trees, everything no longer seemed to loom over me. *Snap!* Instinctively I pulled out an ornate wand and flicked my foreign wrist - nothing. Again, wrist flicked, nothing but a downhill spark. Suddenly, a voice pierced the constricting silence, "Don't worry, it's temporary..."

Nida Alveena Wahab (12)

MISTAKEN IDENTITY

I watch as he flies to save a distressed family from the fire. Congratulations and cheers praise his heroic actions. I glance out from the police van window, waiting to be punished for his wicked actions. Civilians pass by, expressing their disgust at the sight of me. Superheroes were never the true heroes. Their loving smiles plastered on their faces, hiding their dishonesty. Disguised behind the popularity of their overwhelming success, superheroes commit the evil they truly desire, framing and manipulating innocent bystanders. I open the window, closely viewing the fake performance before me. They've arrested the wrong man... again.

Maya Skerritt (15)

DESTRUCTION – A TWISTED SNOW WHITE

Brutes. Grisly, unworthy, petrifying brutes. An eerie silence echoed through the walls. I was tethered. Tethered like a horse with no liberation. Trapped. Defeated. What have they done? My veins pop vigorously. Darkness, the supreme ruler of the Underworld, yet remains. I was supposed to oppose, rule. How could I let this happen? At long last, the curse was lifted. The burden, which ate through my bitter-sweet soul. No. These preposterous, good-for-nothing subjects, captured their last hope. Their queen. They feasted with my enemy. Ungrateful. I was warned. The throne must be mine. I must complete the sacrifice. I'll remain Queen.

Abigail Olajide (12)

A TALE DARK AND GOTHIC

"I still haven't forgotten that you trapped me in my own reflection," murmured Maleficent.

"With you captured, everyone is safe," said Peter Pan. Maleficent grinned and pulled out her necklace. She shouted, "Oh Ultimate Orb, I summon you!" In a blink of an eye, a giant orb appeared and broke the mirror which Maleficent was in. Peter Pan gasped and attacked Maleficent at the same time Maleficent attacked him. When their magic collided, a huge explosion occurred. Darkness corrupted, infusing the world with darkness and sorrows... The only piece that was left from this fight... was the orb.

Puja Ariga

THE CRIMSON PANTOFLE

Gruelling hours are spent sterilising untrodden ruby-red rugs, disguising her nightly rituals, until she makes her unnatural escape to the ball, where she celebrates her felonies. She returns with a deceased forest in the blonde hair she possesses.

Knock! Knock! Upon our chateau's doorsteps, a tribe of handsome guards stands with a noble aristocrat holding a crimson glass slipper (that had a tone of beautiful blue) blinding our eyes. We - Drizella and Anastasia - desperately try to fit the ravishing pantofle but to no avail.

Our sister tries her luck... Jackpot, it fits like a glove. The guards detain her...

George Dixon

JOKER

While Joker took a seat in his outspread hassock he suddenly heard a light buzz. He got up to check what happened and noticed a little boy ringing his phone. "Peter!" he said as he sprinted and answered the phone.

Peter said, "Come to Disneyland, your favourite character is there."

"Mickey Mouse," Joker said.

"So are you coming?" Peter said.

"I'm down," shouted Joker

A few hours later...

Joker and Peter loved it. They took pictures and even brought a teddy. As Joker got home, he was exhausted so he snuggled with his Mickey in his comfy bed. *Zzzzzz!*

Faliha Shaikh (12)

THE LITTLE BOX

"Aw, is little Jasmine going to cry? How weak!"
"Stop it, Harley! This isn't funny!"
"Ugh! This is boring, let's leave!"
As the hallway became fuller, the loud and insane laughter drifted away, filling the poor girl's heart with despair.
Later that night, she awoke in anger and ran to her little box. "I swore I'd never use this," she softly whispered, taking the snow globe out of the box. Suddenly, Harley awoke, freezing and in pain. The ground began to shake. She heard a loud voice say, "Now it's funny." That was the best day ever.

Hollie Smith (12)

EASTER'S ENEMY

The night before Easter, excitement filled the world almost overflowing it. Children, asleep and some not. You're probably wondering who I am... the Shadow Man. The Easter bunny's worst enemy. I never had any type of Easter celebration, so why should others get that 'joy'? Colourful eggs scattered around the gardens. Smiles of children around every corner. Children believing... will all be wiped out soon. All thanks to me. Children will believe in the Shadow Man and beautiful nightmares will overtake their minds at night, they will be looking over their shoulder with every step they take. Bye-bye bunny.

Cydney-Grace Tebbutt (15)

THE SLIPPERY ONE

Once upon a nightmare, there was a preposterous juvenile who cohabited with three alluring sisters. She scrubbed the blood-red floors to conceal her scandalous activities. Her wizard father entombed the ugly one, intimidated by her phenomenal powers, fearful she would overcome him. Daytime was her only nemesis but she was bloodthirsty for fights. She walked around with her solitary slipper. When would someone confront her grotesque features and realise that us, the terrific trio, were innocent of her dastardly crimes? We were always blamed for her felonies and yet they called us ugly. We were her sisters; who was she?

Nathaniel Glascott-Tull (11)

DAMSEL IN DISTRESS

There was one beautiful damsel named Rosaline, every man in the village would come kissing at her feet, magnifying her features, obsessing over this one girl. Strangely, she would refuse every marriage offer, of course, making her parents go ballistic. The village women were jaundiced, bitter people, they despised Rosaline calling her 'the shameful seductress'. Truth be told, Rosaline was lonely and intelligent, she didn't allow her wisdom to be wasted on a man. The village women protested and claimed she was a witch to be hung. Rosaline knew she had no power besides beauty, so fled and never returned.

Moyo Dasaolu

SUMMIT OF THE PUPPETEER'S MURDER

Savage Overlord, Prim Murderer - I go by several names but never by my birth name, Sage. Perhaps my mother hadn't engraved it well on the box she left with seven-month-old me on the windowsill of Sacred Heart Orphanage seventeen years ago. I lived in the ramshackle orphanage for fifteen years, trudging as a marionette of Mrs Parker's avarice. Forced to earn money, I spent daybreaks begging in the unpaved streets of Crestbourne. Oftentimes, I'd go 'home' with sixpence, where my blood-soaked bones are grated upon Mrs Parker's ravenous soul - and yet they ask me why I had slain her bodiless.

Sama Fattah (15)

THE CROOKED ONE

My age was golden. Everything was perfect. Sure, mortals weren't treated too well, but have you seen what they've done to the world? Without guidance they're nothing! You may think I'm cruel but if you were to experience everything I have you would be even worse. My father despised me, and my own mother could not remember my name. I was desperate for validation, recognition, something, anything. Yet after all this, I'm still the villain? You have done many terrible things, mortal. Funny how your kind forgives yourselves so quickly but never others. You have also killed, Perseus Jackson.

Sophie Hawkins (12)

MYSTERIOUS RENEE

I wake up to a stunning morning leaving not a mist in the air but... suddenly, a raging, treacherous storm pounds out of my heart on the blood-soaked ground leaving a red-detailed silhouette swaying to break from netting, wrecking everything in sight. *Smash! Bang! Snap! Crack!* Leaving a feisty nut behind, I run to the rusty mirror, my sobbing changes everything in my imagination. I run out to the crowded streets, shooting crashing missiles out my burning hands, dead-frightened civilians run for their lives. Knowing what I can do, I go rushing to the bank. "Finally, the time has come..."

Amina Kanwal (10)

ORIGIN OF CRUELLA DE VIL

Troubled mind, only influenced by her manic mum, born into a family of dreadful hunters and pure-blooded killers.

Her mum calls, "Morning. Deer for dinner?"

She knows something bad is brewing in her mum's deadly head. She drags herself into another terrible day, a crushing weight of expectation on her shoulders. She trembles down the cobbled staircase, freezing her soul.

Her mum penitently waits at the bottom with a rifle. A bang fills the room. She scurries back up the stairs. Echoey taps only begin to get louder. She lifts her rifle and shoots her mum, satisfied with the result.

Frederick Hanlon (11)

IDENTIFIED

I sensed the impending danger prickling down my spine.
"Put your hands up," bellowed a menacing voice. Everyone's
focus bolted to the door where a masked figure stood with
a gun directed at my head.
"Give me money or the boy dies."
Mama looked at Papa warily, tears flooding her eyes.
I tried to clamp down the fear that threatened to paralyse
me. Papa had to say something soon or it was all over.
A gunshot shattered the silence. I clasped my eyes closed.
"Jason - my son," Mama shrieked looking at the bloody,
pierced body of the lifeless gunman...

Shakir Moledina (13)

WHY ME?

It's sad we couldn't get along, it's their fault.
Never will I forget the day when they took my life from me.
They came and took everything, piece by piece.
I take my revenge on those who took it all. But they think I take everything, day after day. All I want is everything back, the way it was before.
'Heroes' they call themselves, 'Saviours' they call themselves, lies, all lies. The so-called 'Heroes' are villains to me.
They make me suffer and it's time they feel the same way as me.
Decisions, decisions. Shall they suffer instead of me?

Louise Thomson (12)

THE LOST STEPDAUGHTER

Cinderella completed everyone's chores, perpetually up to my standards. She did everything! Consequently, I don't know where to start.

She never wanted new clothes, quite selfless really. When she wasn't working, she was away with fairies. She always received gifts from her parents as though she was queen. Then the prince falls madly in love with her, so she's really queen now.

She never opened up to me, maybe her parents' deaths shocked her too much? If only we'd become close. Although it's too late now. I do miss her but it's as though she died alongside her parents.

Lola Byatt (14)

THRONE

The secondary had stood at the precipice of The Greater Evils for much of their malevolence.

The primary did not stand. He sat, atop his skeleton throne, the apex of calamity.

The Greater Evils reigned dominance over the many lands and the secondary grew ever attentive to their failings. Why fester in malignant ignorance to the naturalistic absence of serene possibility? The secondary shifted, then she plunged the blade into the primary's spine, severing his stability. She stared at the empty throne, skulls red with the blood of the abuser, and thought, if anyone, who should sit in it next?

Edwin Brown

PLANET PURGE

Ever had a dream, the worst one? What if that was real.
Planet 5152. A creature unlike a human stepped on the
ground, crystals coming out of his head, orange and purple.
"Hear me and rejoice. You're about to die in the hands of
space. Before you ask, it was time travel. You found a way.
It's destroying space creating multiverses. Your pitiful planet
dies." The creature's arms rose up and orange-like dust was
coming to his hands. Buildings were falling apart slowly until
everything collapsed. Everyone, dead. Time stood still. The
planet, scorched by heat. The purge had finished.

Aidan Wilson (13)

NEVER BE PROUD

I was a hooligan, a monstrous immortal with no purpose in life. I was labelled as a foolish, menacing and useless child of an adulterous god and a scorned goddess. My existence was loathed, for I was the god of war: Ares.

I've always carried a sliver of regret concerning the countless unethical choices I've made; decisions that caused my rapid descent into bloodthirst. I hadn't cared at the time, being a youth desperate for love and recognition.

"All I want is to make my father proud." I'd decided.

"Nothing else matters."

Zeus had never and would never be proud.

Jael Fisher

HELL TO HEAVEN

Why does everyone fear me? Talk about me like I'm the one who made the monster 'I am'. Tries to tame me like fire when they're only eagerly fuelling me. Try containing the oppressive heat I emit from the flames, the thick heavy smoke suffocating lungs in a blistering embrace, the burgeoning heat, silencing bodies' hearts. Even water couldn't mellow the torridity. Nothing can and nothing would. Because it wasn't my anger or shame that was the villain, nor was it you. I'm the Underworld, made to persecute the sinners of Earth, but that doesn't make me one of them.

Maliyah Lucas (15)

CAPTAIN HOOK

Tick-tock. Another one has arrived. *Tick-tock.* Peter's at it again. *Tick-tock.* Another life is gone.

That blessed crocodile always knows when another soul has entered Netherland. It knows every child who has ever walked these never ageing hills and swam in these forever beautiful springs.

I'm Captain James Hook, and my work has just begun. My whole life I have wanted to sail the seas, I never wanted to come to this godforsaken island. I never wanted to save the children, whom that boy kidnapped.

This is my story and many before me. A story with no survivors...

Gabrielle Rice (13)

THE DREADFUL TRUTH

Malicious, cruel, ghastly! That is all they see in me, if only they knew... I used to work in an ancient charity campaign to help old, sick people, but no one cared if I did. People said I was dreadful and horrible, and that is when everything changed. "Mal, Mal, Mal," screamed my assistant, Tale. "What?" I roared.

Tale looked at me in disgust and looked down awkwardly like he was hiding something. "The king i-i-i-is sending g-g-g-guards to come and kill you," stuttered Tale in misery. My terrified heart began to pound, knowing that they will never care.

Mahrosh Zeeshan (12)

WHY ME?

Me... all they do is blame me. After all, was I the one wanting them to go through hardship? Twenty years stuck in this diabolical world. Have they nothing to look up to about me? All I ever hungered over was repayment and privilege. They turned me into this unpleasant monster. Aren't superheroes supposed to save people from danger, make an individual's life, hell? So, who's the real villain? It's always 'Batman saves us again' or 'Batman, our hero'. If only they knew what really happened between us... then, I'd be their hero. I will seek refuge from them!

Laiba Naved (12)

THE PAST COUPLE OF YEARS

People blame me for everything these days, honestly, it's rude. I didn't ask to be created. Everyone is saying they're tired of hearing about me; I'm tired of people complaining about me! Like I understand that I've caused a lot of heartbreak over the past couple of years, but it's not like I'm able to control myself. If I could, I would. I don't cause pain on purpose. I've changed people's lives for the worse and the guilt eats me alive. Sadly, I probably won't ever completely disappear. Life is changed forever. Know, I would go away if I could.

Maddison La-Ragione (14)

SOMETHING SUSPICIOUS!

Once there lived many blood-curdling vampires, all devoting their days to killing innocent mammals. However, the other side of town was populated with humans. Nobody ever left their homes, fearing these spine-chilling vampires, though some wonder whether these beasts are a myth or not. How would anyone find out without exiting their houses?

In a cottage lived a usual and normal kid named Aiden. Days went by of watching television, eating, sleeping and maybe a game. His parents knocked on his room door. They were going to a party.

After that day there was no sight of Aiden's parents...

Riyam Banitorfi (11)

ANCIENT GREECE

In ancient Greece, specifically Knossos, lived a misunderstood 'monster'. Theseus heard about it and he came to Crete to destroy it. Theseus trudged through the endless maze until after three weeks of searching tirelessly, he turned a corner and there it was... the Minotaur. Theseus wielded his sword and ran up to the beast. The Minotaur ran but Theseus kept up the chase. The Minotaur turned around, dipped its head and its two horns went straight through the hero. The Minotaur sat down and began to cry. He wished somebody would understand that all he wanted was to live peacefully.

Harvey Onions (14)

BRIAR ROSE - FROM THE VIEW OF THE THIRTEENTH FAIRY (MALEFICENT)

Broken. This morning back at my house, I found my broomstick broken. But who would do such a thing? The king. He's always favoured my twelve sisters. Maybe he'd even know where they went. But, it's really hard to find good quality broomsticks! Riddled with ire, I walked. Soon enough, I arrived at the palace, where the front gate swung open for them. I caught a glimpse of the glaring truth. The palace party's missing puzzle piece - me. Eldest of my sisters, yet uninvited. Rejoicing dances grew silent upon my entrance, as a baby princess cried. My sisters' voices broke.

Hafsah Bint (12)

NO ONE COULD EVER LOVE THE VILLAIN

People were staring. "I'm innocent," I pleaded; my bloody hands tied. If only they knew... But nobody believes villains. He held a knife to my neck. "Am I her hero?"
She told me she'd love me if I did it - nobody loved me. He shook his head. "What she wanted wasn't yours to give."
Silence.
"I'm the bad guy?"
"You always were."
I broke the ties and grabbed the blade. They thought I would go for him... but, there was someone I hated more. I pushed the blade deep into my chest. It was over. I got my happy ending.

Twisha Pradhan (13)

LISTEN

She always knew it would end up like this. Everyone else might have overlooked it, but if a child has to go through those experiences, there's very little hope left for them in future.

You might see her now, casting spells, causing havoc. It could've easily been avoided if only someone had listened to her.

It's too late now, too late to turn back the clock, to apologise, to stop.

It's too late to listen.

The happiness she could have had as a young child? It's too late.

The help she could've gotten when it was needed? It's too late.

Zainab Kamara (15)

UNFAIR

"Life isn't fair." That's what Mother always said when she was poor. Doubt she would say that now she's married some rich man. Now she'd say, "Don't work, just rest." I wish! 'Cause my sister and I are having to do what she says more than we usually have to lately. But her commands are much sillier and way more impossible than ever. Especially with a stepsister like her. Her dad always loved her, and she was so spoilt. However, she's become a maid for my mother. Serves her right. But now I must marry Prince Charming and show Cinderella.

Zoe Wand (12)

SEEN

He gets everything. For what? Being a hero? Rubbish. I could've been a hero, but the world never sees me. Why? Because one mistake defines me.
"You will not be seen."
"You're a disappointment."
"You'll never be a hero."
I made a mistake. Nobody let me redeem myself. He made several mistakes but he helps people so that's seen as okay. I am done. I will start to become seen, even if it's a way that people will hate me. They'll see me as the 'bad guy', even 'the villain' if you must. I don't care. I will be seen.

Amy Alexander

DECEIT UNDISCERNED

Aggravating child - elicited in misery. Birds hum - a tune of warning - you pay no mind... foolish. Venturing into occultation, expectancy high. All I've done, discarded behind. Common sense abandoned after your convergence. Opalescent eyes seek his lost in avaricious clouded eyes. Cohabits with the Devil does he. I - a mentor - have given a mother's love undeservedly. Take it when your heart is borne for display yet annihilated by the hero you worship. Move on, we'll see yet you shan't be my burden to bear for I raised him hence discern thy lunacy that taints him...

Sibgha Saeed (14)

THE TWISTED TALE OF HARLEY QUINN

Harley Quinn wasn't all bad, she never wanted to be growing up, but she had no choice. Her sister made her go through the floor, killing her inside. She was the cruellest to Harley, making her do things she never wanted to do. Telling her she's nothing. Harley always said no but her sister threatened the most horrible things like, "I will twist your evil-eyed teddy's head backwards," or, "I will ruin your favourite fantasy storybook." After every threat, Harley felt she wasn't good enough, that she should do all these dreadful things, or be bad...

Holly Archer

GRANDMOTHER'S FOOTSTEPS

"What happened to my grandmother?" Ellie asked questions, and got few answers. The atmosphere would turn coldly sinister just by the mention of her. Ellie started searching for answers, over the years nothing more she could find out. Until one day whilst sitting in the park, she finds a newspaper on a bench. A black and white picture of herself looked back at her, this was a page she'd soon wish to forget. The headline read: 'Serial killer of 22 children, released after 50 years'. Her world changed, answers flew at her with all the questions she had ever asked.

Eve Murray (16)

THE OFFICE

I hear them as they are dragged into my office. Cries, weeps, wails; nothing I haven't heard before. They are helplessly pushed in front of me, shaking and shivering. The look in their eyes screams over and over: "I'm going to die today." They try to run, but I trap them. There's no escaping now. I turn around and grab it, the sharp point edging closer and closer to their sweating and slimy skin.

"Calm down, puppy. It's just a vaccination," I say to the dog.

"Don't take it personally. She's never liked the vets," the owner says.

Sophia Chapple (17)

POWER DOWN

Tightening the final screw, I stepped back and marvelled at my stunning creation. The robot towered above me, its glimmering fists twice as large as my head. I flicked a shiny lever, and my invention waddled speedily out the doorway. Using my robot's X-ray vision, the superhero's lair stood in plain sight. One swing of its colossal hands will transform the lair into a cascading pile of rubble. But, when my victory was mere seconds away, the power went out!
The robotic legs bent before crashing towards the ground, the head faceplanting only metres from the lair. I had lost.

Zachary Colling-Blackman (11)

MRS COULTER

The click of her heels echoed down the empty halls of the Magisterium. She strode past high doors, symbols of the Authority etched on them in gilded wood. Her golden monkey stalked beside her, casting suspicious looks at every door. She reached the grand double doors which stood between her and the power she desired, symbols of the Authority stretching across the wood. A ghostly smirk flickered across her lips. She raised her fist to knock, and the sound echoed soundly throughout the corridors. The doors swung open, and Marisa Coulter stepped into the heart of the Magisterium.

Fergus Hebbert (14)

THE CALLING

A cloaked figure glided into his room, shrouded in mist, a slender scythe clutched in skeletal fingers, the rest of the body concealed in cloth. From atop his bed, the boy looked up and his breath was snatched away by what he saw; the blood draining from his ghost-like face, his phone dropping from his hand onto the floor below. The humanoid shape moved to him, scythe raised, poised to strike. There was a scream from downstairs, and the figure hurriedly tapped him on the shoulder rasping, "You're safe now." He was transported to a place beyond his wildest dreams.

Jacob Christie (10)

PERSONAL SACRIFICE

It's lonely living my life. I spoke previously of their sacrifices that purified this world, the things I had to do. The 'crimes' I 'committed'. Now it's time to tell of the sacrifices I made. After my parents disappeared I never bothered to interact and make friends, keeping a distance was easier work. There was one person. A girl, about my age, who was the purest of them all, she embodied the perfection I wanted for this world. I let her go, secluded myself and made that sacrifice to fuel my motivations. So that others could have their pure world.

Shauna Cowley (17)

SUPERNOVA

Supernova is about to start his machine and cure all diseases in the world, however, the core of the reactor is getting overloaded and will explode. Supernova is worried about what will happen but explains how his machine is to end the world altogether as then diseases won't spread without caring that diseases can be cured and not cause everyone to die. Just before he sets off his machine the reactor blows up killing hundreds of millions of people with between 6-7 billion people left alive. Supernova's body is left in the rubble yet his eyes beam open once again...

Elliot Yensen (12)

RUINED

I did it to survive. You must understand. Sometimes your actions are irrevocable, and yet sometimes they are the only thing standing between you and your downfall. What you do is more important than what you say, and after years of practice, you stop caring about the consequences. If it helps you to live, then it's worth every second - even when the thing in question is so horribly twisted, so utterly soul-destroying.

After all, the price of living is guilt and shame. Guilt, shame and all sorts of other emotions. It was always me or them. And I chose myself.

Sophie Jones (15)

WHAT IF RAPUNZEL'S PARENTS WERE EVIL...?

Rapunzel went about another day in her parents' palace. Things had been a little dull lately and her parents had been acting off. Of course, I knew why, the maids know everything, we hear too much. Rapunzel's parents burst through the door.

"Here we go," I whispered under my breath. They had told her. They were selling her into marriage. Not only would the young girl be forced to marry, she would have to leave Flynn too. If only she would've stayed in that tower far, far away, in the depths of the mystical wood where harm couldn't reach her.

Sallie Sykes (13)

THE MISJUDGED VENGEANCE

As I trudged through the misty suburbs, I observed an unfamiliar occurrence. I almost fainted with ultimate shock. It was the man who'd convicted me of a misdemeanour. I felt a sudden rush of revenge flowing through my veins. I walked stealthily towards him; my machete clenched robustly. I spun him around and he studied me with utmost paranoia. I slashed my machete across his jugular, and he dropped down, surrounded by blood. Coincidentally, I was hauled to the ground as shackles were chained over my wrists. Behind me, I heard a vociferous roar asking me why I did it.

Tanveer Ahamed

SCAR'S TRUE SELF

I spotted my cherry-red nail polish lying in front of my skincare supplies while I was combing my hair. I started painting my nails right away. I decided to put on my coconut-scented mask as I waited for my nails to dry. As I began braiding my hair, I slipped a grape into my mouth. Afterwards, I put a pair of cucumbers over my eyes. "Scar!" Mother yelled. "Dinner is ready!"
"Hold on, Mother!" I spoke. As my eyelids grew sleepy after eating, I slipped into my pink and white polka-dot comforter before I felt my consciousness ebbing away.

Annum Iqbal (12)

A VILLAIN'S BACKSTORY

Tenko? Never heard of him, Tomura? Yes! Tomura Shigaraki, birthname: Tenko Shimura.
Power: Decay. He's stereotyped as a 'villain'. Yes, he may have committed several crimes but mentally, the real villain is his father. The one who tortured him and his elder sister, mostly him. It all went down when Tenko turned four, it started with his dog, then his sister, Hana Shimura, then everyone else. The one that hurt the most was his mother, before she crumbled and dissolved into thin air she tried to hold her son in her hands one last time before it ended for her.

Evita Lleshi

REFLECTION OF A VILLAIN

Ever heard of mirror, mirror on the wall? Well, that's me. I only wanted to kill Snow White and the Evil Queen was already twisted enough, she just needed a slight push. After all, who did she come to for advice? Reassurance? I may seem like just a fragment of glass, but I know the one thing stronger than love; jealousy. I would've succeeded if it wasn't for that darn prince. Now my 'poor' queen is running from their revenge! It was all too easy, really... No one stares long enough to realise that there's something wrong with their reflection...

Shannon Mussell (14)

LOVE AND WAR

"It was you, you killed him!"

"My sweet, sweet girl, as far as I am concerned, it was that arrow that shot through his heart that killed him, not me." Her confused words were only a hindrance to my big plans. She doesn't need to know that I was the one who ordered the arrow to be fired. "I am the goddess of love, why would I destroy something so fickle and sacred?"

"My lady," she whispered, vengeance and bitterness dripping from her words, "I think you forget there is a thin line between love and war."

Freya Quinn (13)

THE GIRL WHO WAS SECRETLY POISONED

There was once a witch who disguised herself as an ordinary person and really wanted to do something evil. It was the princess' 16th birthday coming up, so she thought, *what can I do to kill her?* The witch brewed a potion. It was called 'True Love'. It was finally the day of the princess' birthday. The witch disguised herself as a dressmaker from the village. She wrapped the bottle up. The princess was given a perfume bottle. She was curious what it smelt like. She sprayed it and dropped straight to the ground. Will the princess ever wake up?

Sofia Joiner (14)

INNOCENCE

The sun's shining brighter and everything's calm and collected, much contrast to what I'm about to do. I'm about to kill, murder Little Red Riding Hood, Grandma and the Hunter. Indeed it's not of integrity but roll with me here. I've been contacted by the Big Bad Wolf asking me to kill them. He claimed after defeating the wolf, they were proclaimed heroes and accepted the offer to live in the castle of the town. Now here I am, tiptoeing through the hallways and into the living suite, where the trio sat on the floor. I raised my innocent axe...

Beryl Hang-Yau Lam (12)

TWINNING IT

"Don't do it!" Those were the words he'd heard far too many times. Don't do what was his question. Most seemed petrified of him, a man who did nothing wrong...
She knew the reasons for those words. After all, she was the reason why. She was the dead twin, conjoined by the hip, the doctor believed that he could 'fix' them. Too bad she had to die. However, there were moments when she took control of him when she made them pay.
Sometimes he had blank gaps, where he remembered nothing. Nobody understood his condition and yet she understood.

Bethan Powell (12)

AM I A MONSTER?

Red was scattered across my cheek. My hands were bloody, and a bloodstained knife was in my hand. A rosy blush spread across my face.

"Why are you doing this?" they shouted at me. They should know why, why I killed all the people that they loved. So that they could have me, and only me. My clothes were bloodsoaked and I looked down at them.

"Because I love you," I said. "Do you love me too?"

They looked at me with anger in their eyes. "Nobody could ever love you, you're a monster!"

What? Am I a monster?

Indya Kelly (12)

MURDER MYSTERY - OR IS IT?

"No! Norva, don't. It's not worth it!" She begged me not to do it, but it was too late: I'd already loaded the pistol and shot. That's when I saw Nicole silently cry: cry of fear, cry of guilt; cry of shame.

As days bled into weeks, the news of James' disappearance spread like a life-taking virus and Nicole was the one who had to take the blame. The one who was accused: she was already labelled as dangerous and threatening. But I knew something they didn't. Something I wouldn't dare tell anyone else. I did it... out of jealousy.

Nyma Jawwad (11)

TWISTED TALES

"I still haven't forgotten what happened that day, the way he did it. He murdered my parents. I can still see the blank expression on their faces stained with crimson blood flowing like a river. It was my vow to find him and bring him to justice. I was cast away as a disturbed child, set aside whilst progress grabbed me by the neck with nobody to guide me. So, I got my hands dirty," said Thorne, the most primal criminal in the world.

PC Farah questioned him, "But how does that link to you eating your victims?"

"Pure Evil."

Guy Perry (13)

MIDNIGHT MURDER

I never really belonged. This world never accepted I was a part of its lush valleys and bustling cities of life. Some had reason to live, whereas I had reason to steal the life from their helpless bodies. Each time my grisly scythe swiped, my stone heart became a little colder, a little darker, a little lonelier. Every bitter night as the stars stared shamefully and the moon shielded its rock-strewn eyes from what was to come, I'd creep outside and strike. They'd be glad to go and leave this heartless world. Nobody cared, really, I'd done them a favour.

Amelia Bahrani (11)

FUGITIVE

Let me back you up. My name's Toby Howard and I'm sixteen years old. I've just been found next to a corpse holding the murder weapon. I've been reported to the police and I'm now two streets away. And there goes the siren. I'm running down Frazer Gardens, knocking down some gnomes on some guy's driveway. Obviously, I did not commit murder, but then, all the blame always goes towards people my age. I hear the siren again. I'm hurtling down an alleyway filled with rubbish and tin cans of soda and then, I'm a fugitive - to the law.

Aryan Nair

ONLY ONE EVIL STEPSISTER

Hello! I'm Annabelle. I've got one sister (Gretel) and one stepsister (Ella). My mother and Gretel are cruel to Ella, whom they call Cinderella. Gretel is the younger sister and she wants to marry Prince Charming. I want a normal life, but Mother has other plans. I'm just a 13-year-old who wants to help, I'm not appreciated. The gruesome twosome (Mother and Gretel) planned to steal the prince's crown and blame Ella. I warned him and now Ella and I are friends. My life is better now that I moved to the countryside with Ella and her grandfather!

Maya Dworak (11)

LOCKED AWAY - MOTHER GOTHEL

All I desire is her hair, the way it would glow as the lyrics escape my lips. How my fingers would flow through it with each word.

"Flower, gleam and glow."

If she doesn't know that she's the reason I look this young, it will be okay. The hair is long enough to last a couple more years. That's all I need.

"Let your powers shine."

Each passing day, her curiosity about going outside of this building grows stronger. What would I do if those people take her when she's out there? What if the truth gets revealed?

Maisie Wilkinson (13)

THE EVIL QUEEN

The cool blade pierces his skin. Blood trickles down his sweaty body as the blade digs deeper and deeper. *Thud*. He falls to the ground. She stands victorious while staring at him lying lifelessly as the sound of the wailing police cars grow louder. Her first kill. And it felt... incredible! The screams of torture, the cries of pain. The whole experience, it was all so thrilling! He deserved every bit of misery. He should have seen it coming his way after he murdered my precious, sweet father. He did nothing. So, long live evil. Long live The Evil Queen!

Lily Blowers (12)

REVOLUTIONARY EVIL

Anastasia was gorgeous. Her existence fed my desire. Drowning in the depths of her tears, she gasped for breath yet allowed for the waves to swallow her whole. Honey kissed eyes lay at the bottom of the lake. Snowflakes grazed the tip of my finger before the warmth of my skin melted them. The snow gave me away. Alyona was uncovered. Raskolnikov was watching. We shared a murderous glance. I couldn't breathe. I felt sick. With one stab he sent me flying. I was with them, the angels, Anastasia, Alyona when I suddenly dropped. I wasn't welcome in heaven.

Lilia Rebihi (13)

THE BIG 'BAD' WOLF?

The everlasting continuous sound of writhing agony drained my soul. She dresses in a blood-red cloak to hush up her callous secrets. She prowls through the dark depths of the murky swamps, whilst I track her fake aroma, simply wanting to expose her real identity, her true self.
Yet I am to blame for her perpetual felonies? I aspire to earn back my respect, therefore I schemed my revenge on this monstrous disappointment to our society.
People have spread vicious rumours for centuries, making 'me' out to be a fiend.
When will you realise, I am innocent?

Mikaeel Keyaan Hussain (11)

FOREIGNER

I covered my mouth with my trembling hands. Fury wasn't enough to describe the emotion churning in my abdomen. My property, my home - licked up by the inexorable inferno. That building had been a part of me. I was born there, raised there; I even graduated in that house. And now it was gone? No. No, it couldn't be the end. It shouldn't be. And what about my children? A pair of vigorous hands seized my arms and cuffed them behind my back.

"You're under arrest for illegal immigration in the 1990s."

I froze. Hadn't I been born here?

Feyisola Ogunsaju (12)

THE DARK MENTOR

There he was. My arch-nemesis/student had returned. He wanted revenge. He could sense I was here. I had to make up for what I'd done. I always knew this would happen. But my plan was in motion. Surely he couldn't stop me now.
"A barakimah dalashi!" I screamed. Jets of black shadow and blue fire shot out of my hands. He was dead to me now.
"Akabora sin hel!" he incanted.
I counterattacked it with the same spell. I turned into a shadow and continued punching until blood gushed out from his throat. Never mess with me...

Ibrahim Karim Sangarie (11)

THE STORY OF DEATH

What is the worst thing you can think of? Your TV breaks? You get stung by a wasp? No. Think worse. Death. That's me. Miserable Death. Every day, people wish that their relatives could live a bit longer. It's my job. So I'm going to strike. Their world will become crowded and sad but do I care? No.

It's been two years since I stopped. I hadn't felt excitement until today. I heard something, an elderly woman's voice. She prayed, "I'm ready to go. I want to leave space and food for my family." Wow! I guess I am wanted.

Alice Walker (11)

BETRAYED

I did it to survive. It was the only way. Everything changed, everything hurt, everything affected me. I was different now. I was overwhelmed, distraught, full of pain. A facade was always put on when it came to meeting me. The person I had most trust in left and betrayed me. That's what hurt most!

My nemesis had returned! Disaster would strike, problems would occur and most importantly, chaos everywhere you looked. My heart ached in agony. There was no escape. I was stuck. The city would rebel against me. I was alone. Now it was time to save myself.

Hanna Khan

BROTHER?

I hear the cries of humans as their 'liberator' plunges his sword deeper through my heart; the warm blood trickles down the blade to its hilt before staining his hands crimson red, but the people only cheer louder. The irony of it all. It's hard to believe this man standing before me, cold in his gaze, used to lovingly call me his sworn brother. Who would have thought that the one for who I became the Devil would be the one who played God. "I carried your crimes, and you purified them with my blood. Was this the plan, 'Brother'?"

Maria Binoy (15)

GOTHAM'S VENGEANCE

Edward N. Journal. 30/10/19
It will be Halloween tomorrow. I'll start my improvement on
Gotham city. This city's in shambles, corruption at every
corner. I will improve this city, people will look at me as a
hero, who rid the streets of corruption among the people we
trust to run this city. I have four main victims, and some
other people, that just annoy me. Our mayor just lies and
lies. After he is dead he'll lie still. The DA, Gil Colson, he
works with Carmine Falcone, Bruce Wayne, the rich orphan,
no true orphan is rich. And finally, everyone.

Devan Babbra (13)

AN UNPLEASANT VISIT TO THE SHOP

My stomach rumbled like a volcanic eruption. I'd forgotten my lunch at home. I trudged towards a shop in the corner with nausea to buy a sandwich and a drink when it struck me. I'd also forgotten my way home. I grabbed a drink and a tuna sandwich innocently before shoving them into my bag undetected. It was a great counterfeit. Suddenly, the manager approached me, his eyebrows furrowed. I shuddered. With an elevated voice, he demanded I open my bag up for inspection. I reluctantly gave him my silver necklace and he happily strolled away with a grin.

Nimarpreet Singh (12)

A SAINT LIKE SATAN

I have to save her from them, they hate me, they don't understand what you wanted to achieve. I was going to make Germany great again - greater than ever before. I can't let her suffer the consequences of what I've done, when I'm gone, they'll come for her. My love. We can go together and live in tranquillity in the heavens, where God will forgive me for disobeying him. He'll understand when I tell him my great ambitions and he will praise me. There my name will go down in greatness: and I will be the greatest... Saint Adolf Hitler.

Olivia Monk (14)

PAN'S TREACHERIES

You may think that Peter Pan's good, he's not. It's not just because I'm Captain Hook, there's another reason besides him chopping off my hand.

When I was a child, my best friend was a merman. We grew up together, then Pan came along! Our precious daughters fell in love with him. He took them away, breaking my friend's heart, killing him. I went after Pan to try to get her back. We began to fight, my daughter flew towards us. I was distracted, Pan cut my hand off in her view. This devastated her, making the dust stop working...

Jasmine-Ann Chambers (13)

JOHN, THE GRIM REAPER

Hello, my name's John but you might know me better as 'The Grim Reaper' or, in a less formal way, 'Death'. Now, before you get mad at me, I think you should be thanking me right about now. Why? Well, isn't it obvious? Without me, people wouldn't die. People would be in excruciating pain and never be able to get out of bed if it wasn't for me. In terms of dying of old age, people would shrivel up more, their memory would worsen and they would become increasingly sick. What's the point of being alive if you can't live?

Andrew Carroll (12)

YOU ONCE LOVED ME

She was my girl. My lovely little girl. My Rapunzel. I'll never forget the day she left me. Darkness draped my life. Cutting her glistening golden locks was the worst thing I've ever had to do. An icy, hollow curtain of dread seemed to silently follow me everywhere I went. I needed her beautiful golden hair to survive. I need her. Her smile, warmth, the way she chuckled and her lopsided smile. I've raised her since birth. Everything came crashing down, cocooning me in something: guilt. I wanted to keep her safe. To protect her from evil I knew.

Adaya Moses

THE ONYX QUOKKA

They called me Onyx. Unimaginative, but they were useless. They'd never seen a dark grey quokka before. They caged me and people came to gawk. At first, it was great, they loved me! Soon I was old news, and nobody cared. I wanted to be alone. The other quokkas would always smile, through rain or shine, but I'd given up hope. I never smiled anymore; I was the grumpy outcast. One feeding time, they didn't lock the cage: I escaped! They almost got me, but I clawed out their eyes. I've been blinding humans ever since. They're all enemies.

Sophia Dobson (12)

BITE OFF MORE THAN YOU CAN CHEW

On a dreary winter's night, my shy toy poodle Benji and I trudged around the local field as the menacing clouds hovered above. A beefy chap barged towards us, his German Shepherd licking his lips ready to pounce.
As quick as a flash, the dogs were having a whale of a time, activating their turbo engines as if powered by Duracell batteries.
In time we split them up and sneakily we strode off the field with a notion of nervousness. "Let's go and get some succulent steak for your dinner Benji with our brand-new wallet," I hissed cheerily.

Charlie Evans (13)

PRESIDENT

I need to win. I'm going to win. Years of nationalism I've spoon-fed into the minds of my people have curated a concoction of radicalisation, which will ensure my opponents' demise. This will be my 14th year... 14th year of prideful dictating. However, it's dawning on me, I'll never be able to secure an untainted victory. I can rely only on tarnished gold, to earn the favour of the bold.

Most yearn for me in that chair though... I hardly see the issue, but I can't help but feel obsolete - pathetic even. I need to win. I will win.

Lara Patel (13)

DEATH AND HIS NEVER-ENDING GOODBYES

Death didn't like his job, but he had no choice. It was always the same; someone's timer would run out, Death travelled miles to collect their soul, they got scared and died of fright. Personally, Death would've rather lifted their soul away, not scared it out, but what could he do? It didn't matter that he was a caring young boy with a gentle smile. The moment he said his name, they screamed. Of course, a millennia of this and Death changed; he's now the creepy, crazy-eyed old skeleton we all know. So when you die, don't scream.

Kristen Judd

THE FALL FROM THE ASTRONOMY TOWER

It was for my father. So I'd be loved, actually loved. I never wanted the stupid mark on my left arm. All I wanted was friends. Real friends like Potter and Granger, not like Crabbe or Goyle. No, this wasn't the life I wanted. But now I stood before my idol on the astronomy tower plateau, staring into his entrancing, azure eyes that always twinkled. I had to kill him. Or my father would get to me before *he* could. However, a braver man stepped forward. Emerald green sparks slithered slowly out of his wand, my hero falling and falling...

Dylan Edwards (12)

JOKER'S JOURNEY

"I was driving in my car, looking out for my enemy, Batman!" said the Joker. As he was driving he saw a familiar-looking car in the distance. It was the Batmobile. As the Joker edged closer he suddenly saw a pair of headlights. It was Batman! The Joker spotted a bat-shaped grapple zooming towards him. The grapple broke the windscreen and narrowly avoided the Joker. But when Batman retracted the grapple it went flying back to him chopping Joker's arm off in the process. As Joker wept in pain he realised that it was the end of his journey.

Joshua Williams-Davies (12)

THE PURPLE BIRTH

The weather seemed to detect that something was amiss the day of the birth, for even the sky, so often a rich shade of azure was coated with thick tufts of cloud. Rain hammered on the immaculate glass that made for the hospital window. The birth was a painful one, as the baby, they declared, was larger than it should be. Yet the sheer size of the newborn was far from being the main concern. The baby was purple. "Isn't he beautiful?" The father's words seemed empty to the mother, who couldn't help but gaze in horror at the child.

Sienna Fraser (17)

LITTLE RED

"Food, food, food there must be..." Suddenly, I saw a girl with a red cape skipping along the path.

"Excuse me miss, can you help me?"

As she turned round, I spotted a savoury-scented basket of food in her hand. She told me her name, Red, and asked how she could help. I explained that all I wanted was some food.

Unfortunately, she couldn't help me because she needed the basket of food for her grandmother. Red told me where her grandmother lived.

At first, I didn't know how it could help me, but then... I had an idea!

Tilly Byatt

MALEFICENT: THE MARVELLOUS MISTRESS

It was a normal day in the moors - the creatures playing in the swamp and Maleficent gazing down upon them. She was the queen - everyone knew that. Everybody feared her, and she liked it. But nobody knew of her secret life - of her normal, non-villainous side. She slipped down out of the tree she was perched in and took off. When she landed, she was in a mystical forest full of beautiful flowers and dandelions. She picked one up and blew gently, watching as the seeds dispersed themselves. She would relax here all afternoon. This was her secret life.

Salina Mobeen (12)

SCARRED

"Prince Christopher, you home?" There was no reply, then suddenly I heard the creaky floorboards behind me. All of a sudden I turned around to see a tall silhouette standing in the shadows, the next thing I knew was I was trapped. His hands cuffed mine, I somehow wriggled free and I tried to fight him, his wand struck my hand leaving a scar in its place. Up from behind Prince Christopher knocked him out with a frying pan. I finally saw that man's face, he was Umbrian, the one and only wizard. "Thank you, Prince Christopher!"

Kira Riley (11)

NOT A TRUST WITH SIGHT ONLY THOUGHTS

Victims and attackers. There is a famous writer who wrote a story. There is a girl who walked by. A sight, without a thought, thinking someone is bullied. Without a trace, not knowing the situation, she quickly helped him who was crying. Later on, the girl was bizarre. She saw the bully and the boy was arrested. She asked her what happened and could never forget what she said, "He was a wanted criminal. Just because someone is weak or bullied, without thinking and only trusting your eyes doesn't mean that they are always the victims."

Lucky Gu

THE RED WOLF

Laughing, I pirouetted with my subjects. Unexpectedly, I felt my hair grow. My clothes burst. Trying to scream, I snarled instead, shuddered and arose from my nightmare.

I meandered until I saw a red-hooded girl burdened with a woven basket. I tracked her to a timid hut. Pouncing through the window, I was in. I put on the clothes of my former snack and waited.

She burst in, "What big teeth you have, what big eyes you have, what lovely hair you have!" I smiled. She screamed. I leapt at her, teeth ready. Then a slice.

Darkness descended...

Aoife Walsh (12)

THE AUTHOR

I can't do this anymore, can't watch these idiots make every mistake. I can't. I've been stuck on the sidelines too long, telling other people's stories. Now, now it's time for my story, but not yet. Not until they're gone. Every single one of them. I'll rip them apart for what they made me do. No. Even better. I'll trap them, somewhere far away from everything. They'll have no choice but to watch as my world and my story lives on. Just as I did. Then, and only then, will I finally get my happily ever after.

Lauren Mitchell (14)

WHEN DARKNESS FALLS

The smell of rabbit was overwhelming. I skulked through the trees, knowing that even the snap of a twig would warn my prey of my presence. The moon cast eerie shadows around me, making me feel small. I inched forward; waiting for the right moment. Finally, when the timing was right, I pounced. My long, fox claws pierced the rabbit's skin and the warm, wet blood spewed everywhere. I began to chew the fur around the pink ears. I heard whimpering from behind me and saw a young kit, clearly my prey's child. Then, I realised what I had done...

Kyla Barney

DEAR DIARY...

It's me again, I thought I would tell you since you're the only one I have been able to talk to after my mother died... Today I finally got revenge on my father. After years of him experimenting on me. My father was preparing his next experiment, I shape-shifted into a mouse and knocked over one of his potions, which exploded! I couldn't see anything because of the explosion. After a bit, my vision came back. The next thing I saw was paramedics rushing into the room... From that day on, my father didn't do experiments on me again.

Maisy Clint (11)

SUBJECT 1130

Subject 1130. Her name was Minerva. She created something too dangerous to exist, it meant she had to be killed.

Many knew her story, yet none survived to tell it... except me.

Last year, she created what they call a 'time machine'; the consequences of creating it, and who she was, are unknown to them.

They destroyed her, and took her kingdom, to protect Earth... right?

You see, the story you've been told is a lie. She was never the villain. And she is alive. How do I know? Because I am Minerva. And I'm here to reclaim my throne.

Ruqayyah Aziz (14)

WRETCHED CAPTAIN HOOK

Remorse fuels you. You knew what Peter Pan's intentions were, yet you decided to risk everything to save the children. What did you get in return? What happened to your arm again? Everyone knew Peter Pan wanted children to stay forever young, but you knew that he was only doing this to claim the world as his. When you told those of Neverland, you were beaten and betrayed by your own people. Ironic isn't it? Regret is your second nature and all you hear are screams that fathom in darkness. Now, no soul knows the truth. Not a single soul.

Alice Faulkner (13)

OUR FRONTLINE HERO

As I sit and gaze at the misty moonlight over the mountains I wonder. I wonder why the world is such a contradiction. We are surrounded by natural beauty, spring is blossoming and yet we are in the midst of a world pandemic, something we can't erase is devastating relatives, killing family and friends, we don't know where it came from or where it is going, or if we will ever return to normal again. Human kindness shines through. We owe you - our frontline worker - you give us hope. This time will never be forgotten and neither will you.

Malaika Kitheka (12)

THE WOLF'S REVENGE

I did it to avenge myself; I had to. Grandma Karen always taunted me in front of everyone, making me the biggest joke ever. She'd always embarrass me somehow but now it was my time to shine.

One day I waited for the nasty old woman to take a stroll in the forest. I hid behind a towering tree, ready to launch apples at her. Bullseye!

I hit her right in the face, making her the laughing stock. She wasn't impressed.

Hunters appeared. Rifles loaded. I ran, but they found me. *Bang!* They shot me!

Vengeance flowed through my veins...

Zahir Alam (12)

MISGUIDED

I wasn't always like this. At one point, I was going to be one of the most beautiful people in the world, then, disaster struck and I became a hideous monster. They call me 'The Queen Of Hearts'. What an ironic title. I'm usually nicknamed, 'The Queen of Broken Hearts'.

All I wanted was for my mother to love me as much as my sister, so, I did something dangerous to prove myself. And it went wrong. All because I wanted love. Well, get ready, Alice dear. The Queen of Broken Hearts is coming for you. And I'm not sweet.

Ellie-Jayne Scott

HE WHO MUST NOT BE NAMED

Everyone has sympathy for the boy who lived, with his jagged scar and emerald eyes. They fail to realise that I was once a boy much like him. I was an orphan too, trapped in an orphanage with people that hated me. They antagonised me simply because I was different. When Voldemort came to take me to Hogwarts it was like I found my home. However, more and more muggle-borns and half-bloods arrived, reminding me of the muggles who tormented me in the past. That's when I decided that all Mudbloods should be eradicated, they weren't like us.

Eloise Moody

JUSTICE KILLER

The blood drips from her pale hands onto the rocky pavement that lies underneath her trembling legs. The blue flashing lights shine on her teary face, the face of pain, yet somewhat pride. Four lifeless bodies of their own blood. She raises her hand, pointing the gun at her head, as she pulls the trigger she takes her last breath, the bullet enters her brain killing her instantly, and her body drops to the ground. Now her lifeless body lies in a pool of her own blood. But one question remains. Why is she a killer? What's Jane's story?

Lauren Neighbour (16)

VAMPIRES ARE NOT EVIL

I can tell you that all except one vampire have a reasonable answer for why they kill.

One person was doing experiments, it turned him into an unbearable monster. He was known as the Beast from Under. These other people never lost themselves. They were able to control what they did. They would only have a litre of blood each day. But once every three full moons anyone in Hunt Mountain was in danger, every vampire would be drawn to Hunt Mountain. There are myths that the Beast from Under rises again and draws them into him at Hunt Mountain...

Ele Pike (16)

VENGEANCE

"What made me choose villainy?" I'm always asked that question. I chose it because of revenge. Before my villainy I was a kind toymaker, then the 'hero' Red Bow (Paul Gray) fired me from my job even though I was the best toymaker there so I became the Twisted Toymaker. I've always been crazy in the head so I made toys into bombs. The only problem, Red Bow's always on my tail. Every time I set my toys on people's houses he's always there. On a busy bridge, he was there stopping my plan or so he thought...

Brandon Gadsby-Cooper (13)

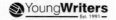

MY ENDLESS TASK

My story has been written in stone a thousand times. They know nothing. I crossed over the bridge, silent as a shadow. Animals fled and my heart sank. I do have a heart, no matter what everyone says. I reached a cottage and the sound of wailing drowned out my thoughts. The curtains were shut, but the door opened. A body lay on the floor and the family looked at me, terrified. "Please, please," they babbled. I beckoned one finger and the body rose. They screamed and I turned away, shaking. I try every time, but this role is eternal.

Jess Porter (13)

BROKEN LOVE

"Do you regret it?"

Do I regret it?

An elegant figure covered in blinding beauty appeared as if she had descended from heaven. She cast a majestic aura from her head all the way to the tip of her broken wings. After being alone for all those years the useless gods finally recognised me; until the gorgeous beast appeared beside her. So, I did what I was born to do. We both had warm scarlet blood drip melodically off our clothes whilst her crystal tears fell onto the lifeless corpse in her arms.

I *DON'T* regret anything!

Nahla Salim (13)

VENGEANCE

My fists clenched, digging my nails into the palm of my hands at the sudden flashback of her murder. A simple kitchen knife was used to torture her to death. Hailee's eyes wide; unable to see, her mouth open, but failed to scream. I still haven't forgotten the gory imagery - how could I? I witnessed perfect health and most importantly, bliss. He doesn't deserve to smile, so I'll watch it fade as though it never existed. I've waited for this moment for years! For now, I'll enjoy my view while my plan falls into place.

Gurman Kaur (13)

MIRROR, MIRROR ON THE WALL, WHO IS THE MOST MISUNDERSTOOD OF THEM ALL?

Told of a curse that would destroy everything the fairest girl touched. I took responsibility and locked myself away until Snow White came to life. Knowing her lack of responsibility, I made a harmless apple that would put her to a temporary sleep. Soon, the curse crept up and like planned, nothing was destroyed. When she finally awoke, she commanded my death. I ran, tripped over a rock, and ended up on a cliff's edge. As I scrambled to hold on, a shoe stepped on my hands. My last view, the smirking face of the one and only Snow White.

Aavni Rao (12)

THE MISTAKEN MURDER

Night. Thick and black, though the moon was banished. The charred remains of a church stood silent. An icy winter wind cut through me, chilling me to the core. Shivering, I closed my eyes, inviting the cold to engulf me while the muscles in my face strained with the intensity of my thoughts. The memories flooded my head - memories of her murder. Tears fell, freezing like rivers of ice into the cracked lines of my wizened face. Frozen like her spirit many years ago. I had to come to visit her. But why was my name carved into the tombstone?

Tasnim Sheikh (13)

SMAUG'S TWISTED TALE

I come back to the day my mother was murdered. The day the dwarves did the ghastly deed. I was brought up by my father. He taught me how to steal and then how to guard the treasure from everyone so that (hopefully) one day I would own a dragon's hoard. Then, I heard about the dwarves' treasure.
Revenge.
Silently, I flew down under the cover of darkness towards the mountain. A stream of flames shot out my mouth. Screams erupted all around. Flames lit up the night. Confusion reigned. In the blink of an eye, the hoard was mine.

Emily Sanders (11)

MYSTERY GIRL

Dexter, our border collie, was pulling hastily towards the entrance to Whites Wood. However, he pulled me through the stile far too fast, throwing me into the path of a girl. "Sorry," I quickly blurted out, but she just looked at me and smiled. A few steps later I looked back, she was still smiling, Her long black hair blowing in the breeze, I smiled back. We continued along the path. Dexter paused for a sniff, I looked up and read a missing poster for a girl that had been missing for ten years. It's the girl I bumped into!

Jacob Haynes

THE JOKER'S SMILE

I was different, Mother said. I stood out. Special? No, just different. Joker is my name. When people from Gotham see me, chills shoot up their spines. Pure fear. They are just simply dramatic. I killed a few people, so what?
As a young boy, I never smiled. When I did, it looked like I was frowning. When frowning, I felt joy. Mother said, "Lighten up!"
At the age of fifteen, I cut either side of my mouth to look happier. Then ran. I ran far. Clown make-up for a disguise. That's when I felt happy. I was the Joker.

Olivia Terrell

MY DEAR HEROES

Redemption and forgiveness can no longer scrub the sins off my hands. Pride of my humanity ditched as I shake hands with Death. Holding a bouquet of lilies, laughing at cries of pain, dancing on the graves in a little black dress.

Why is my confidence cursed and your pride praised when your ego runs louder than mine? Selfless and selfish come from the womb of one mother. In this narcissistic world, nothing we do can ever be noble. If truth lies in our beliefs, your words are the bible and I live in the chapter of the fallen angel.

Lynn Guo (15)

BRING BACK WHAT ONCE WAS MINE...

Brushing Rapunzel's hair seems like a simple thing, worthless to many, precious to mothers, but to me, it is more than that, it is the only way I can remain young and beautiful. Of course, many would consider this evil, cruel, even vicious. But is it really?

My whole life has been wasted into something truly awful, and now I can be young again, live life again. As I listen to Rapunzel singing, I feel pity, I feel somehow proud. I think this is called parenting, yet I remind myself that this is fake. Maybe even my life is fake.

Maya Valero Teuma (12)

SOOTHING...

The violent storm flooded the small village, yes there weren't many people living there but there was one unknown castle that sat in the corner of the village collecting dust. It was eerie and isolated, no one at all dared to go there. The wind whistled around the ancient trees. Black silhouettes were lurking in the corner, you could hear children crying and wailing but this wasn't the most terrifying or menacing thing ever. It was Maleficent. Her cackles were so loud the village rumbled, her yelling was the most intimidating.

Zainab Safeer (12)

THE HOOD

Twisted. That's what Little Red Riding Hood is. I'll always remember that day, sunny and not a cloud in sight. That is until she joined her grandmother and me for tea. I've always been friends with her gran but that girl is evil and despised our friendship. I thought she was starting to like me but I couldn't have been more wrong. Sipping my tea I realised a smile was growing on her face, that smile grew bigger and more evil as the world started to fade around me. I woke up being arrested for murder. She's twisted.

Jessica Mallett (14)

THE TRUTH OF THE THREE BILLY GOATS GRUFF

Hi, I'm the big ugly troll from the Three Billy Goats Gruff, but you can call me Bernard.

One day, I heard annoying little hoof beats above me when I was trying to make a lamb roast. So, I came to see what was going on.

Three goats stood before me. Naturally, I yelled, "What are you doing on my bridge?"

They stumbled back in fear because I didn't sound very thrilled to see them. Then, they all stampeded towards me. That's right, all of them.

And I fell into the fast-flowing river, butted off my own bridge. Rude.

Amber Antoine (10)

MYSTERIOUS NIGHT OF HALLOWEEN

It was Halloween when it all happened. Tim was walking down a foggy and gloomy street. Suddenly, Tim saw an intimidating figure running towards him. The figure looked grisly and eerie. Tim was spooked and rather than running he weed his pants. This made the abominable creature laugh at him, but then a man from behind came and knocked down the gruesome creature.

Tim helped the man to murder the creature, but soon he realised that it was his father who came to pick him up. Tim looked at the man next to him, and he got his macabre back.

Vipul Jain

DAMIA'S THOUGHTS TO CONQUER

I think it's absolutely ravishing when someone begs on their knees. It makes me feel just marvellous when a devilish little soul even dares to mutter a word, I simply crush them down lower with my foot and they beg for their life.

I think all humans are a waste of this alluring planet... Earth. So brainless like chickens, but hey ho, they are fun to play with. I just know that one day I will conquer it, and they will all be begging and chanting my name in despair... "Damia!" Oh, how glorious and triumphant it will be...

Diala Farmer (17)

DARKNESS FALLING

The darkness was falling, and the stars were twinkling above the heavy treetops. A perfect way to hide and wait for people making their way back from their Christmas parties, all full of food and stinking laughter.

Will I get the chance for revenge on the people who bullied me when I was younger, that mean daily group who walked around the school thinking they were perfect. They hurt many people and now was the time for them to feel this pain, that has been buried inside. We are all here to stand together, to entice them into a trap.

Archie Robinson (13)

PRINCIPLES OF VENGEANCE

I never thought I'd be in the position I was in now. The cold steel of a knife felt weightless in my hands. Such a simple tool, yet so effective. The blood and gore spread across the concrete floor created an almost picturesque scene of utter destruction. I felt no remorse, nor should I. He'd been a cruel man, ruining others' lives for his own personal, monetary gain, selling other people to support his luxurious life, but it had ended, his last sight the strange grin I held as I plunged the knife deep within his jugular.

Maison Steele

WEASLEY THE WITCH

So now I'm dead. I wasn't the real villain. So what if I supported Voldemort. One day they will realise that Mrs Weasley was a traitor. I loved James Potter. I watched out for him and then when Harry came along, I watched over him too. Mrs Weasley had to be stopped. That was the reason I started the fight. Harry's safety was all that mattered. The only reason I tried to kill Harry was to make my cover secure. Harry chased me and I almost killed him! I must go now. The connection from the otherworld is unstable. Farewell!

David Swales (12)

GREY THANOS

"I can still remember the day you beige humans came to Earth. I was thirty when you came, and you slaughtered my world. I escaped by chance, seeing you stab my friend in the heart. The last seconds of his life were in pain. In rage, I tore my hair out. I hate looking like a human - at least I'm violet. When you went away from my home planet, I allowed myself to fall asleep in an underground cellar. My first thought was to kill all humanity, for they'd given me so much emotional torture... I will have my revenge..."

Leon Ridey (11)

ATTACK ON MY ATTACKERS

My plan was in motion. I was ready for the next lot of my attackers but were they ready for what was next? The zombies were trapped inside the cages. My next victims, running through the doors. The zombies were unleashed. I heard the screams of fear and cries for help but watched on paralysed with excitement and happiness. It felt like forever since this last happened; I was longing for my part. I lured the zombies back into the cages as I ran toward the frightened people. I never liked thinking of them as people but as the enemy...

Caitlin Banfield (14)

OUTCAST

My plan was never to end up like this - destroying everything I got my grubby little hands on, but then again I didn't like the way I was before either. Life gets hard and when you can't stand yourself I'm not sure how you're supposed to like anybody else.
It became a small habit of mine: making a friend, becoming the only person they need and then one day destroying it all. It gave me real satisfaction to see their little faces go from elated to distraught in a matter of seconds. It's not my fault I was ruined.

Sydney Edwards (15)

DARK KNIGHT

I never forgot the day my parents were killed. Growing up, I was never told why my parents died. My parents discovered the truth behind the superhero group and were going to publish it the day they were murdered. I remember clutching the dead corpses of my parents with streams of tears breaking free from my eye. The group emerged out of the shadows and taunted me. I was powerless. That day I swore revenge. You can be sure I will not rest until everyone that killed my parents is dead. You can run but you can't hide. Dark Knight.

Leon Anish (13)

STARING DEATH IN THE FACE

Like a cornered animal, the man below was trembling with raw fear. Only he could see me. He knew it was over. His family surrounded him, desperately saying their goodbyes. Upon his dying breath, I entered his body. My mind was flooded with memories and experiences. I had taken over... They call me death. From the beginning of time, I had existed with solely one purpose. To take over the world one body at a time. When I find a body that is suitable enough to die, I take it over efficiently and methodically. Eventually, I will win...

Muhammad Akhtar (13)

THE MASTER

I've been wronged so many times! I have views for the world you see. Big views. I imagine myself on a throne, ruling over Time Lords. Nobody would be safe from my rule. Not if the wretched Doctor had anything to do with it! Now, I'm stuck here, about to be thrown into the time vortex. I'd be erased from history, a punishment worse than death. I cannot let it happen. I'll escape. They knew I was coming. They desperately tried to stop me. So many poor innocents had to go. They thought it was worth it, they were wrong.

Jamie Peacock (12)

REPLACEMENT

I never wanted to be the villain. I look around at the destruction I have just caused, collapsing buildings and children's cries filling the streets, my heart aches. I didn't want this. The people used to love me, they built statues of me and wrote poems of my heroism, that was until he showed up... I didn't know I would end up being the villain, that I would destroy the town I swore to protect. What else was I supposed to do? They were going to replace me. I couldn't let that happen. I only wanted them to love me.

Katie Mitchell (16)

THE ONLY WAY

His angry nature and persistence to slaughter my kind, drove me to action. I've been trying so hard to resist violence but he's hunting me, I won't get out alive if nothing is done. For years, trapped; threatened by mankind, it's time for revenge. As I crept up behind him, the hunter spun around and jabbed me with his spear. I thrust my hands towards him and tore off his arms, leaving him dead in a veil of blood. I lumbered off into the forest, disgusted and consumed by guilt, but I knew that it was the only way...

Alana Pope (15)

DON'T PLAY WITH FIRE

I've always loved fire, but my father hated it, the house was always cold and so was he. I would make my father light the fire every night, I was mesmerised by it, it looked so free and I ached to feel like that, I wanted to be fire. "Don't play with fire," he would say. My father hated fire with a passion. "Don't play with fire," I laughed as I reached for the matches, gasoline in one hand. He looked so peaceful when he was asleep - he didn't look as cold-hearted. I wanted him to be warm.

Eva Taylor-Williams (13)

THE DARK DREAM

In my dream, my father's voice whispered to me from every direction imaginable. I wanted to let it go, since the day it happened I could not accept how he had passed but I knew he was gone. I could sleep whenever I could hear him whispering to me but sometimes it didn't feel right. My father had always been a good man but the things he said, I almost felt like he was pulling me in, somehow, with words, somewhere... Then it happened, I awoke. A scintillating light beaming in my eyes. Beeping sounds all around. Where was I?

Oscar Meek

SNOW WHITE - A TWISTED TALE

Grimhilde stood seething, with a grimace plastered over her face - how dare the mirror lie to her. She was the most beautiful of them all. After all, she had made a ludicrous bet with the witch and sacrificed it all to be beautiful. In other words, to be loved. She stood awe-bound to the mirror and asked it, "Who is the most beautiful of them all?"
And the response she got was worse than if she never asked at all. Snow white. The daughter of the backstabber herself. She wasn't going to let history repeat itself...

Mariyam Ali (13)

DINNER WITH JANET

I never really belonged; it was hard when I was a kid being cast out by everyone for who I was.

Twenty years later... My family still haven't talked to me since the troubling incident. I skipped over to the kitchen, eagerly pulling the fresh meat out of the already packed fridge, tossing it onto the worn-out counter. The oil drowned the meat as I did to her. I tossed it onto my warmed plate. As my fork pierced the juicy bloody meat, Janet tasted nicer than who she was.

I did it to survive... You would do you same.

Libby Goode (13)

CONTROL

Crimson-red blood stained my hands, her last words made me smile as the knife I plunged through her chest went deeper and deeper. Then an exasperated shrill woke me from my trance as I saw the only thing I love... gone. Drowning in her own blood just like I drowned in my own actions. A monster is what she called me. That... thing inside of me taking away everything, anything that I love. I felt like I couldn't breathe or be free, unless I let that thing, that monster completely take over me and let everyone pay for my pain.

Nadine Pedrick (14)

ARABIAN NIGHTS

On a cold November night, as the east wind howled across the desert, a pitiful cry was heard from a Bedouin tent. Warm in his mother's embrace, a child was swaddled into his nomad family. As the sun rose over the dunes, a battle cry was heard, the child was taken whilst his family were left for dead.

The infant grew up in a world of thievery and despair, learning his trade as a pickpocket on the streets of Agrabah. He spent his evenings on the rooftops, gazing at the Sultan's gleaming palace, plotting his way to power.

Amelie Putt (12)

DARKNESS OF DEATH

Rage undulated its way through my veins like a snake, poisoning the opaque ruby-red fluid and tainting it with a rich shade of jade. Suddenly, my firm grip tightened more around her ivory white neck. I could feel her heart pumping, beating so heavily it could quite easily burst through her chest at any moment. I could sense her fear. I could tell her breaths were becoming shallower by the second. I could see her life slowly slipping away into the darkness of death. I felt no remorse. I did it to survive. It was my only option.

Lucy Harris (17)

THE GRIM STORY

I'm as old as life itself. Older than death. People complain about their job or the work they must endure. I assure you, my duty is worse. Perhaps some people are afraid of lawyers, any type of person with a job that gives authority really, but almost everyone is afraid of me, my job. I don't know exactly where the fear of me came from but as always, people are afraid of strangers and things they do not understand. I work every day, some are sadly more busy than others, you might say I work myself to me. I'm Death.

Lucia Baker (14)

PUTIN - I'M NOT A PUNK

They have no idea what they're talking about. I want to be known. I wanted to be looked up to, acknowledged, and seen as someone of power and authority. I thought annexing Ukraine would help me attain that. I never intended for it to go this far. I want to stop, but don't know how. I don't want anyone to know, so I give up. I continue to show people that I'm strong, but I don't have time to change. People already hate me, and I can't do anything about it. I don't want to admit it, but I'm sorry.

Caroline Newton (12)

THE STORY OF THANOS

I couldn't believe it. The darn Avengers had turned me to dust. The five of them attacked me, maliciously attacked me out of nowhere. I travelled to different planets to ask each of the Avengers for the Infinity Stones. I first asked Tony Stark for a stone. He transformed into Iron Man right in front of my eyes and blasted me into next week! When I asked Steve Rogers for one he threw his shield at me. When I asked the Hulk he smashed me. Black Widow shot me. Finally, Thor launched Mjölnir at me and turned me to dust.

Chulu Feni (14)

A FRIEND FOR ME

In you come stranger, abandoned, left alone, not anymore, yes, yes, take the bait, walk up to the front. I will have revenge after they took my mother away, my mother, my poor mother, sick, she was sick! And they took her, all alone I was, betrayed, but finally a friend, hopefully, they like me. Walk into the opening doors like the opening arms of my mother when I was down. Here I am, glued to the cameras watching him like a hawk, judging the paintings I saw, the pictures of the nuns he didn't like, don't be scared...

Harley Crossman (13)

PTSDEATH

It's hard you know. When I, an eternal entity, signed up for the role of Death, I thought it would be easy. Just turn up, reap some souls and be on your way. But no. They don't remove your emotion, they just let you deal with it on your own. I'm not afraid to admit, so many times I have wished I could reap my own soul, take my own life. Nobody mentions having to take a grandaughter's life whilst their grandma watches. Having to listen to a child calling, concerned, for the dog it doesn't yet know is dead.

Isobel Heald (13)

LADY TREMAINE'S HAPPY EVER AFTER

I'll never forget what he told me that day on the beach.
"I love you so much. I want to marry you someday."
His words kept playing over and over in my head like a song on repeat. But the next day I woke up, he was gone and didn't say goodbye. I later learned that he got married to another woman. They have a daughter and I have two daughters, Anastasia and Drizella. Their daughter's name is Cinderella. His wife died when their daughter was five years old. I will never forget what he did to me.

Ruby Pike

ONE'S DUTY IS NOT ANOTHER'S RESPONSIBILITY

When I was a child, I thought Christmas was a time for families to reconnect, share memories and overcome future difficulties. That was until I was abandoned by my parents, who thought I was worthless. How is my appearance my fault? Isn't it the time of year when we take the time to appreciate who we are? The love of a parent is the greatest gift they can receive from their parents. When I was born until now, I didn't receive that from my parents... How can it be given to these people? What do they have that I lack?

Kamsana Kalaivasan (15)

INVISIBLE ENEMY

She never sees me, except in a mirror. I run around after her, mess with her mind in the dark. Sometimes, when she's in pieces on the floor, I like to tease her by giving her the wrong pattern to join herself together again. I like to tell her she is who she isn't, I like to keep her back from being all she was made to be; to keep her believing she's worthless. She'll never get rid of me. I am her shadow. I am the voice in her head. I... am... *fading* because she isn't *listening* anymore.

Leonie Hanan (14)

RUBY

Black silhouettes stormed past. A girl stood there, waiting. Her ruby coat floating in the wind. Her face, pale as a ghost. Then she ran. Fast. She stares right at you. You see joy and laughter in her eyes but mischief in her body. She reaches out and you are stuck. Then she says, "I never really belonged. I never will." And she releases you. You fall down. Down. Down. Down. And you realise - this is all your fault. You did this to her. And death is the price that you have paid. And revenge was what she had done.

Jessica Edgar (12)

THE EPILOGUE OF JM

I watch you from afar. I am always alone. You don't see me even though you were my best friend. You are with your family, and you look happier than I ever remember. It is snowing and it is freezing cold, but I don't feel the winter chill... I feel nothing. You'll be okay now... my distant colleagues and I made sure of this. You have saved a child's life and in one day helped so many. We always knew you had a heart and could be redeemed.
I saved your soul Ebeneezer Scrooge, now who's going to save mine?

Garry Cunningham (17)

THE VILLAIN INSIDE ALL OF US

From when you watch a scary movie to when you turn off the light for bed, he lurks everywhere. He creeps up on you when you least expect it, then entangles your brain like vines on cobbled streets. He is under your bed and outstretches his hand. His fingers, cold to the touch send a shiver down your spine. All the information gathered is that he is never truly gone. The identity of the mysterious figure is that he is the fear that comes from within, and he never retreats, only creeps in the shadows away from public view.

Faye Perry (12)

THE ENDERMAN'S ORIGIN

I never really belonged to face this pain, this... suffering. The atmosphere in this strange dimension poisoned me, my eyes turned purple, my skin turned blacker than the midnight sky. I was sent to this dimension, what they call 'The End', but I had to adapt to fit the dangerous gasses. But they ruined my life, my family, my friends, my everything. I was stuck in here forever. It wasn't until recently that it all added up. I, the Enderman, had my good life taken away, and now they must pay, I needed revenge.

Christopher McComish (13)

THE HOOK-HANDED MAN

I did it to survive and look where that got me. While that flying idiot kills innocent kids to stay young, I'm stuck in this wretched place with a hook for a hand. My crew have been here for years, yet they still haven't given up hope. Hope. The thing that can save you yet gets you killed. Everyone thinks that he's the hero, but little do they know that the lost boys don't go missing in action. They get killed by the one they love the most. Peter Pan. I, Captain James Hook, swear to take this menace down.

Ella Shani

CRIMINAL REMORSE

Dark, immoral and malevolent, all words to describe a common criminal but did they choose this life of crime? We are about to find out. I am a criminal, a very common criminal. I do the basic stuff... robbing banks and pickpocketing but people seem to stereotype us criminals. I never wanted to become one but I guess it's the only way to survive this cruel world. When I make these poor decisions, I think about whom I may be hurting or torturing from the pain of my choices but I guess that's the life of a criminal.

Mariama Nyallay (14)

I DID IT TO STAY ALIVE (FOREVER)

As a child, I was always more gifted than others, but I had one fear, and the day I found out I was a wizard I knew I could finally overcome it. My fear was death, leaving the world and its wonders behind. After doing much research, I found out that there was only one way - Horcruxes. Everything I did, including the murder, was to stay alive. Some people like Harry Potter were just in the way. They could've left me to it, but no, they didn't. They decided to stand in the way of Lord Voldemort, which was foolish.

Roxana Anderson-Cristea (12)

TO FORGET WHAT IT IS TO FEEL

Absence of light had deprived me of my senses but when the relief washed over me, it wasn't long after until the guilt did too. Guilt carries weight that many other emotions do not. It is a motivator, a possessor, a source of drama and judgment. Many are ignorant, but those who view guilt in the light are the ones who have truly forgotten what it is like to experience the fear that comes with it. I was drowning in the truth's embrace and as my story came to a close, I realised that I was the villain all along...

Aksa Ahmed (16)

I HAD TO MAKE UP FOR WHAT I HAD DONE

I grew up in happy Whoville. I lost my parents. I struggled without their presence. I felt cold. I was mocked, teased and alone because I was different. I fled to the hills. I learned to hate Christmas. I became grouchy, grizzly, grumpy. My heart shrank.

One day, I found a friend who didn't give up on me - Max my dog! We caused havoc in Whoville. We broke. We controlled. We stole. They were sad: sad for me! I gave it all back and my heart grew. I felt worthy. Were they all so bad? I found the Christmas Spirit.

Millie Graves (13)

THE REVENGE

My mother, Bellatrix Lestrange, and my father, Lord Voldemort, are dead. Both murdered. I want revenge. I will hunt them down one by one, using one of their own. I will not rest until Molly and Ginny Weasley and the famous Harry Potter are dead! My name is Katana Lestrange and this is my story. You may think you have heard or read this tale before, but I can assure you that this is nothing like that. Read at your own risk, for this is not for the faintest of hearts. My story begins at the end of Hogwarts' Battle...

Lucy Daw (14)

FIRST CONFESSION

"You haven't slept for a while, Kuhisa." Lizzy looked down at his sleep-deprived master.

Kuhisa sat up to stare then opened his mouth to speak.

"I once had a best friend, he lived in a lighthouse beside the island I considered my home. When we first met, I was frail and weak, no milk to the bone. He did not mind me. Though I prowled around on all fours not much like today, he considered me no less than a brother. He opened his arms to me and with a ravenous look to my yellow eyes - I ate him."

Alyssa Cupid (15)

PANDORA'S REVENGE

Everyone knows the girl who carelessly released all the evils and miseries to the world, but my story isn't known. Created by Zeus, being gifted with extreme beauty and kindness and used as a punishment for Prometheus who stole fire to give to man. Later to marry Epimetheus. Am I the villain of the story?

Zeus' plan to use me enraged me. Stealing the present given on our wedding, I released all the evils in the world, keeping behind hope so that man will suffer the same way I did. In the end, I chose revenge.

Nana-Oye Appiah (16)

MY WIFE

For two years, she never fought with me. It was true love. But one night, it all changed. "I'm sorry, the trip's only for a few days! Promise I'll make it up to you!" She had never left me before. Who was she going to see? Another man? And just like that, I realised that my wife was gone. I was devastated. Clearly, if I were to preserve her memory, to hold on to that precious angel she once was, something drastic had to be done. And so, I got rid of the despicable thing that had taken her place.

Toni Agbede (17)

IT'S YOU OR ME, PREFERABLY YOU

I handed Snow White the apple from my small wicker basket. Her beautiful, soft hands hugged the apple perfectly, she was hesitant to take a bite. Snow White was so full of life, soon she would be so full of death. The apple edged closer toward her and a smile walked slowly onto my face. She stopped and reached behind her, pulling something out of her dress. She pushed it towards me and it sank through my skin, crimson blood slithered out of the wound like escaping red snakes. It was me who was full of death, not her.

Kiera Crouch (13)

THE FALLEN ANGEL

The Devil was once a fallen angel. Crying, on his knees, for forgiveness. And that moment had changed him, ripped him of all senses and left him powerless and vulnerable to the judgement of others. Everyone believed that he was not capable of love, that he had no heart. But there is more to a person than what meets the eye. Because the inside wounds can never be seen by those who do not wish to see it. The Devil was so broken, beyond repair, that not even the sweetest lies could lift him out of his endless suffering.

Piranavi Chandrasekaran (13)

POOR LANGUISHER

My mother told us tales of beautiful sea creatures. I longed to be like them to frolic beneath the waves. I knew the ocean was my only predestination.
One night I finally saw them. Mermaids. They agreed to grant my wish. I was to be one of them!
I entered the water, and they began to chant. I felt a great change come over me, but when I looked it wasn't a shimmering tail I saw, but writhing tentacles! Those wretched mermaids had tricked me! I was a monster! I fled. Now I lurk in this cave, plotting my revenge...

Sahar Ahmed

PESKY LITTLE DEVILS

I am known as the evil witch, but really my name is Piper, not that those ungrateful brats would even remember. Hansel and Gretel are entitled snobs!

They told everyone that I was plumping them up to eat them, but I was simply being a good host. Just because I took one tiny bite, those tyrants threw me into an oven. Pesky little devils!

When I saw them all plump and delicious, I was forced to act. I did it and I would do it again. That doesn't make me a bad person. I am simply misunderstood.

Savanna Puk (12)

MOUNT EVEREST

They want to conquer me. They try to destroy my beauty.
They pay the ultimate price. Many have tried to climb me,
few have managed. The effort I put in to obliterate anyone
who tries to conquer me is absurd. People climb to my peak,
most die before getting there. I'm so tall I go above the
clouds. I'm so cold I'll give you frostbite. I knock down your
temporary homes and rip out your spirit with my icy-cold
breath. I don't want to have to do this but I do it to survive...
Humans devastate the Earth.

Freya Wright (11)

NOT A HERO, NEITHER A VILLAIN!

Don't you want to hear my story? The one that proves me innocent, but hardly a hero. Really, I'm not a villain at heart. I just had no other option. I'm like a lion in a cage stared at by goggle-eyed, ugly creatures that call my jail a zoo. I'm lonely and my heart aches and that makes me angry. So angry. Love doesn't exist. I know that now. But I was naive to let Harper in. She wasn't repulsed by my ugly appearance, except, it was all just a cruel dare. So, she's the villain in my story.

Lydia Alford (12)

A TWISTED MYSTERY

I'm not sorry, I had my reasons. She ruined my life, took the one thing that made me happy away. I was going to do exactly the same to her just as she had done fifteen slow painful years ago. To this day I still mourn my father's death, the events still fresh in my head. She was the reason my father died that night, but nobody saw it that way. Besides Catherine Hilton was the most popular woman in town, the one who constantly organised charity events. Everybody loved her, I did once until I got to know her.

Maria Magalhaes McKown (13)

A BEAST SO CROOKED AND CRUEL

I didn't mean for her to die. It was an accident...

Her dead eyes are vivid in my mind, the way they fell from wide to blank burned into my memory. My knife dangles on the edge of my desk, glinting red in the dim lamplight.

If they want to make me a villain, then I'll give them a villain. I'll give them a beast so crooked and cruel, it will haunt their nightmares and stain their dreams a virulent red. I'll show them the ugly truth. I'll show them. I lay my head on the pillow. Eyes flutter shut.

Ilana Taylor (15)

VOLDEMORT REDEEMING HIMSELF

After I killed Harry Potter, I felt victorious in the moment, like my life goal was complete. But years after, I found out that doing bad isn't the way. I actually felt bad about killing him. So I thought to make it up to his friends. I went into town, to the pottery club. I asked the guy for clay and somehow he seemed shocked. I don't know why. After I received my piece of clay, I decided to make a clay sculpture of Harry Potter. It took a long time to complete, but I'm happy with the amazing product.

Porshad Anooshah

MORTALS OF DEATH

It was me or Kye. One of us would be executed for murdering my brother. I knew it was me. I was mentally ill at the time. The thing is, I have experienced death before. The underworld is a thing, but heaven isn't.
By the way, I'm a mortal. I can leap through different dimensions and travel through time. Although I'm on Earth, I came from a different world, a world where you can live by your own rules. The only law is, you can't go to Earth. But here I am now. My fate shall decide my future...

Harry Harper (11)

THE GREEN SNATCHER

He does it once annually. He rounds up boys and forms an
army of kidnappers. I must stop him! I need someone else to
do the job; I'm getting too old.
He claims he is chasing the shadow of his former good self
but I know differently. He is the son of the wizard. 'The Great
Dardoon' and has been sent to destroy Neverland.
He uses the skin of deceased children in his camp to cover
the old man he actually is. How has no one noticed this?
How does this green snatcher make me out to be a villain?

Max Piercy (13)

REFLECTION

Mirror mirror on the wall, who really is the fairest of them all? I've been painted a fool, wallowing in my self-hatred and jealousy. Young Snow White has the beauty and grace of a dove whilst I lie here, sinking into the ancient palace walls. That apple was cruel, as cruel as the world is to me. A poison curse that disguised my bitter envy. I wait for my prince charming to find me but no. Instead, I'm outdone by a daughter that is not even my own. I am left on my deathbed wounded. Wounded and alone.

Nyra Hernandez

THE LEGACY

It all started when I died. After the car accident, there was no way to save me. I had made one too many mistakes; the only way to redeem myself was to kill him and take his place: an old man. Too old to do his job properly.

The best part of the job is helping people, but sometimes they don't need my help. Some take care of themselves. Sadly. And there is nothing I can do to make it better for them.

I don't want to do this anymore. I'm ready for someone to take my place.

Yours,

Death.

Connie Allen (11)

AN EYE FOR AN EYE

Someone once spoke honest words to me but asked the wrong question just like they always do, "Would you die for me?" And you know what? It made me smile, but it stretched the skin-tight stitches lifting the mask across my face. I could see the liquid dripping off my face before I felt it, so my smile was red and bitter just like the blood, and I could have realised right then that the lies were slowly killing me, after all, everyone's fine with an eye for an eye, that is, until it's their own.

Maaria Najeeb (13)

THE REAL DEAL ABOUT THE BIG BAD WOLF

I'm Wolfy, the big bad wolf I'm sure you've heard of. Everyone's quick to judge! Look at the three little piggies. I blew the house down is what they say. It was raining; I asked them to let me in. They said no but the coldness of the rain has given me a cold and I sneezed their house away! Red Riding Hood... I asked her to be my friend, but she snobbishly turned me down and told her famous dad the story you've heard of today. I have no friends. Many more have turned me down. What about you?

Rital Badewi (12)

BATMAN THE VILLIAN

The whole superhero act was just a lie. Batman is really the villain. He just uses the people to turn on me. It's not fair! I have come up with a plan in which I defeat him. How it works is when he arrives home, I'll be waiting above the door with an axe that will cut his head clean off.
I'm in position. Here he comes. All I could hear were the sound of his boots. Next, it was the sound of flesh slicing. After it was screams of pain. Then, *thud*. Finally, there was silence. Batman was dead.

Sebastian Schönrock (13)

DEATH

I ran, gripping Al's wrist, not letting go. The soldiers were catching up to us. I gripped their wrist even tighter as we jumped into the trees. I wasn't going to let them take Al from me. I pulled Al to my chest and picked them up, running from branch to branch. The soldiers were even closer now. They pulled out their guns and began firing. I was afraid this would happen. The bullets kept coming. I felt a jolt of pain hit me, someone shot me. I heard a scream. It was Al. They were shot, in the head.

Mishel Mir (13)

MERCY

Mercy, they twist the word until it bends to them, fully obedient. Now it's my turn, and there will be no mercy for them. No matter how much they beg and cry, just as they used to do to those who did what they had to survive in this wretched world, that suits our pretty hero flawlessly. Always one to get their way no matter what others need. In the end, that's what made me pull the trigger. That more people would suffer at their hands if they continued to live. All it took was a push, click and bang.

Menaal Khan

AM I REALLY AN EVIL WITCH?

You might know me as the 'villain' since I'm a witch and they are always portrayed as evil. Well, I'm not, everyone always runs away from me, I can barely even do magic. I wish I could, it would be a miracle.
One day, I met this young girl and she asked me if I could do magic. I said yes. I tried and it somehow worked, her mother walked behind me and called me insane and told me to never come near her child again. I didn't know I could do magic... I never did magic ever, ever again.

Isabelle Anderson (12)

HADES' BACKSTORY

Ever since Hades was a child he knew that he would never be loved the same way as his siblings were. So, he vowed to take over his brothers' lives and be the favourite sibling instead of Zeus and Poseidon. He knew he had to overthrow the god of lightning and the god of the sea to fulfil his wish. For some time Hades thought to himself, *how long will it take for people to like me so I can get close to Zeus?* Then it came to him, he should kill Zeus' first child. His journey to success began!

Zahara Ali (11)

THE OPPOSITE

It has always been the same. We've always been seen as the enemies but they never see what's behind us; the stuff we had to see to come to where we are now. But I guess it's always the same. We stand in the ranks with the worst of the people who killed people as today the stone-cold body is in front of me.
As the knife with crimson blood drips off. I've been standing for almost an hour; just waiting, just staring into her eyes. They were so familiar, almost as if they were my own.

Edith Parker-Gerrity (14)

ROBIN HOOD

Stealing from the rich and giving to the filthy poor. Doesn't Mr Hood know that is our hard-earned money that he is nicking! I have to be in a room with stinky peasants to judge their despicable crimes. And that is all down to that Robin Hood! He is a model figurehead for the unclean. Do you know how hard it is not to insult the grim? We rich are afraid to go outside. We could get our valuables taken from us! Why does that wretched thing think he can prance around pick-pocketing? Curse you, Robin Hood!

Bernadette Trimmings (13)

I AM TOM MARVOLO RIDDLE

I will kill him this time. When I kill him everybody will be under my control, his destiny is to die. There is this girl named Ginny Weasley. Weasley huh, ah yes Ginny is the dear little sister of Ron Weasley. She could lead me right to him. The him in question is the boy who lived, Harry Potter. That boy has ruined my life, it is now his time to perish as I did eleven years ago. Harry Potter won't get past me this time. It's been too long since I've been this close to killing that selfish boy.

Seren Mai Williams (13)

JOHN IAN ISN'T WHO YOU THINK HE IS

What if the villain John Ian wasn't actually a sociopath serial killer? Let's find out...
John Ian is a so-called sociopathic serial killer but have you noticed that when he robbed the bank he didn't have the money? It's because he gave it to charity but he still got arrested. Well, he did kill the children so he is still a criminal! Well, he killed them to be able to feed his family. Would you not do anything to save your family if they were dying! If not, you are the true sociopath here!

Lacey Jane Scott (11)

HARRY'S POTTER DEFEAT...

The sun rose high in the sky. I was lying awake planning what I should do to Harry Potter but the thing is that Harry Potter and I have the same wand so that means I cannot defeat him with the same wand. Birds circled around Hogwarts Castle. This is where I learned my magic. I was lying on my bed and then I cast a spell. This spell brings down demons to suck people's souls. As they were flying over Hogwarts I could see that they had already sucked a lot of souls. Their soul-sucking counter was high...

Muhammed Safyan Iqbal (12)

LOSS

I know what it's like to lose a child, but if I returned to the kingdom empty-handed, they'd kill me. It was early in the morning and I had a day off. As I left I waved to the portrait of my wife goodbye and made my way towards the guild. Upon entering the guild, it was silent, an unlikely sight. The piercing looks I received made me nervous. "The mythical dragon's son failed to return, pay with your life." Even though I was afraid, if this dragon didn't kill me, the guild would.

Ronaldo Da Costa

URSULA HAS A LOVELY SINGING VOICE

"I'll see him wriggle like a worm on a hook!" These words still cross my mind, let me tell you what happened.
Mother told me I could be anything. That was a lie. When I heard Ariel's voice, I faced the truth. I wasn't good enough but I knew I had to win the crown, my crown.
So, I did what I do best. I made Ariel walk but in return, I took her voice. King Triton had to pay for killing my mother. Would you do nothing? Would you play by their rules or would you make new ones?

Marta Beirao (11)

KILLER QUEEN

"The world lives in terror after Killer Queen-" I shut the TV off. They don't even use my name. 'Killer Queen', that's all I am to them now. All they see is my past, they don't see how much I want my future to be changed. I'm just the psycho who murdered her family and all her friends. They don't know that my family never cared for me and I did what I had to do. I wasn't always evil, every villain has a backstory, it's just about whether you choose to listen.

Laila Sherwen (12)

NO OTHER WAY

They think that I'm bad, that I killed for pleasure. But they're wrong. There was no other way.
We try to get through our differences, or at least I do, but they still don't understand. I am who I am for a reason. The people who made me like this have paid but they keep trying to make me pay too. I did it so that the people I loved wouldn't die. But they still did. It must have all been in vain, right? Truth is, it wasn't. It taught me how to survive. And surviving is the only way...

Zahra Master (12)

WHAT IS THE GRIM REAPER HIDING?

People say there's always a happy ending to a story... but not this one! You're probably wondering who I am? I am Death itself, the Grim Reaper. I will prove that I am the evillest villain. I've killed millions, if not billions in my time and I decide whether you live or die, either way, I couldn't care less. After all, Grim is in my name. Remember unfortunate humans, if you see a figure dressed in black with dark mist surrounding him, run! Because that's when I'm coming for you.

Bella Ward (11)

HOW DARE YOU!

I don't believe this, how could you, HOW DARE YOU!
All I have ever done is take your murderous, depraved,
scheming, violent and evil people and punish them for all
the havoc they have caused on your world. I have only ever
tried to give justice and vengeance to all of you who have
been treated horribly by such people and now I have
learned that you all see me as the villain?
Me as the evil one?
How dare you?
My name literally means Light of the Morning and you lot
call me Satan?

Millie McEvoy (13)

THE FOUNDATIONS OF EVIL

My parents took me to a dark and ominous forest filled with predators and without remorse, they left me, a child, in the hands of beasts.

It wasn't long till a beast appeared snarling with its grotesque face. But it didn't eat me, it just smiled and eventually took me in. My life changed a lot, to the orcs I was seen as a god with inhumane power.

When I was of age, I became the king founding the great city Mordor and turning the orcs into bloodthirsty beasts. It was time for revenge!

Zakariyah Raja (12)

NO SUCH THING AS WINNING

The self-proclaimed hero had lost, as the villain stood tall. It only took one slip up for this result yet... they felt guilty, every fight before left them on the floor. Maybe it was because of how this hero behind closed doors had a family, a parent, a child, who will find their loved one had perished in a battle that seemed so petty now... The fuss that will be made would never happen if it was them. No one would care, they had no family. It was all for nothing... Yet it felt so right at the time.

Caitlin Tabb (14)

THE TRUTH REVEALED

That superhero act was all a lie but what could I do? I didn't want to be the ship's baby. I mean I know I'm supposed to be the captain but under the surface, Peter Pan is the one to blame. He fed my hand to a crocodile and now if I don't fight for revenge I will be the ship's crybaby, a laughing stock; and that just won't do! You see the crew pressure me into fighting; though I'm truly just a softy. I mean if it was up to me, we would never battle. I would just surrender!

Lucie Edgar (11)

THE DAY LUCY DIED

I'll never forget the day Lucy died. We were in the park, having a nice time. Lucy did a jump off the swing, it was perfect. We went on the slide, but then Lucy tripped. She grazed her knee, it seemed like it really hurt. I went to help her up, salty tears were running down her face. We walked home. It started thundering. Lightning struck a tree and it hit us both. I scarcely survived, Lucy didn't. Today is the day she died, four years ago but earlier this morning, Lucy knocked on the door...

Erin Ghaley (12)

THE RED APPLE

I still haven't forgotten the day when my brother betrayed me. He had always said that I would make a fantastic queen following his abdication. But one day, when we were eating red apples, he told me that he had met the most amazing girl in the kingdom and that they were to be married, meaning she would be queen! She was so precious to him now, not me, all I had was myself, not even a place on the throne in my power. So I poisoned them with red apples: a sweet reminder of the day he betrayed me.

Lillian May Pedley (13)

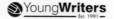

THE PLOT

I did it. I finally did it. They all knew it was them not me. I beat the hero and my name is cleared! How you may ask? Well, it was pretty simple, I planted the evidence on every billboard in town, waited for the Red Carpet event to commence and voilà. Chaos began. Until things went bad on my end of the plot. It turns out that all the evidence I gathered was altered. None of it was real? This doesn't make sense! If I'm not the villain, they aren't the villain... Then who is?

Claudia Mirembe

THE WOLF'S BANDANA

I was the wolf of this story. I wasn't always; but things changed, as they so often do in tales of blood-red cloaks. The witch was evil to her bones. She took me, gave me a home, then cursed me to have a human mind, gave me a red bandana, only to steal it and sew it to her grandaughter's red coat when it got too short. She abandoned me. I attempted to take my revenge but the lumberjack killed me and stuffed me. They gave me to the demon's grandaughter who they then ate. I was the wolf.

Esther Woods (12)

SURVIVAL

I stared and stared at the dead body before me. I did what I had to to survive. He would've killed me otherwise. But that doesn't make it feel any better than it is. What've I done? I have to get out of here. It's not safe for me anymore. So I ran and ran until my home was a flicker in the distance. What should I do now? Start a new life, create a new name? But then suddenly, my heart began pounding, my vision became blurry and the world darkened around me and I fell to the ground.

Emily Edgar (12)

THE TRUTH BEHIND LITTLE RED RIDING HOOD'S GRANDMA

My side of the story is far different from what you all know. Little Red Riding Hood's Grandma was not so innocent herself. I will bring you to the start where it all began. When I was just a pup my mummy just wanted to look after me, but Grandma did not want that to happen. One day I went hunting and then suddenly when I got back, my mummy was not there. All I saw was an engraving on a piece of wood... 'I have her now, from Grandma'. And everyone thinks I am the villain. I'm not.

Emma Boyce (12)

TICK TICK BOOM

He had to do what he had done. He stood still, gun in hand. He pulled the Glock up to the face of a frightened-looking woman. Two bangs went off and a body dropped to the floor. The mysterious figure had a myriad of ideas in his head. He walked over to the body and stared at it. "That's what you get for killing my family," he said with a manic smile on his face.

He then spat on the lifeless body and walked away without a trace. An explosion was heard and the dead body vanished.

Kayla Enamu (12)

THE END

It was only us two now. I knew only one of us was going to get out alive. The arena I was in could only have one survivor. My friends and brother, Mellisa, Shreya and Jason, could both live because of the arena they were in, but not me. I knew I was going to die any second now. "Well Alexandra," Xander sneered, "only two of us now." He grabbed his sword and lunged at me. Just in time, I dodged, reached for my last knife and threw it at him. In the blink of an eye, he was dead.

Eleanor Restell (11)

ABSOLUTES

Here you fight and for what? For an absolute order, for peace and prosperity, for the end of chaos. But, is that what the universe decrees? As I stand before you, I say that you are wrong. As a coin has one side, so must it have another: for order, there must be chaos. To remove chaos is to remove balance and removing that is to create a greater chaos than you can imagine. I am not your enemy, you are your own enemy, for your misjudgement has blinded you to seek the end of the thing you protect.

Ryan Al-Turk (15)

MY SOMBRE SIDE OF THE STORY

The magic I had, was stolen from me, fed to the queen, who fell gravely ill. In my attempt to get it back, I grew to love the child, who was the root of my death. My name is Gothel, known as Rapunzel's stepmother. My children perished in the war. I had no family left, so I had no ambition to live. But then I discovered a flower, which granted me the power to be forever young. However, I was robbed of it. There was only one thing I could do: find the baby girl, whose hair wielded the power...

Haleema Zeeshan (11)

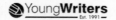

THE INTERROGATION

In a police station in London, a mysterious figure was being interrogated. "I never really fit in anywhere. I was bullied for what I looked like and for how I didn't have a home to come to so I ran away and didn't turn back. Years later, I saw the boys that bullied me and I tore them apart and hid their bodies in a bin. I will never regret it." As he finished, with a sweep of his cloak he was gone, leaving the detectives in a state of shock and leaving behind a drop of blood.

Oliver Campbell

STARS ARE TOO FAR AWAY TO SEE CLEARLY

The disreputable celebrity slammed his hotel room door. Evil reporters. So what if he was drunk on set and ruthlessly beat up the director?! Why didn't all his good deeds make headlines? He cried. Fame and money had ruined and enslaved him. The press had given him a persona he hated. He thought about his pre-fame days, before he became a prisoner. A prisoner with five ex-wives and 9.6 million dollars.

A mean and lonely prisoner looking longingly at the 30-foot drop from his window.

Faith Carter (14)

CHECKMATE

I did it to survive... All the pieces were in motion and the game was sure to be mine for the win. I could hear the gasping of their voices... her voice... I didn't want to lose ever again. Crime seemed to be my only way out of this. I promised to bring her a safe life... and she betrays me! I've done things that I'm not proud of... but to get back on top and claim my last victory... I have to make this city something better but he took it away from me. I'll have my revenge...

Finlie Hynd (14)

THE TRUTH OF LILITH

Adam was infatuated with me at first. He said that he loved me. That out of the whole of the garden, I was the thing he valued the most. His world. His girl. That I was greater than the length of the river's valley, the deer that rejoiced in the woodland, the sun. I was truly the apple of his eye. Then, Eve appeared. And, as the story failed to mention, he loved her more than me. So with my dignity, I left the garden for someone that promised to love me even more. To never stop loving me.

Jaiden White (16)

VICTORIOUS VILLAINS

Finally, I was about to win! Until they found out I cheated! I went to the dog centre to buy some dogs to add to my collection. I came home with five dogs and painted black spots on them. I went to the competition and whoever had the most Dalmatian dogs (real) would win. But obviously, mine weren't real. The man at the competition fair picked a dog up with wet paint on... and got black paint all over his hand and clothes! So I lost, which was very, very, very annoying for me and my dogs!

Maisie Leigh (11)

THE ONES LEFT BEHIND

I am Ethan. I am a 'villain'. This is my story...
A long time ago I was friends with this guy, Clark. We were best buddies! Until... Clark met a stranger who offered him fame and money, but he had to leave me! I looked him dead in the eye thinking he would say no, but no he didn't say! He said yes! At the hero academy, he got all he wanted, money, fame, everything! But I knew the truth. How could people be so blind? How could they not see who he really was?! I had to show them.

Caitlin Clay (11)

A TIMELY END

I was supposed to be the one whose veins flowed with envy and betrayal but now crimson spills onto the ground that I lay on. Me, always second best, trying so hard but just missing the goal whilst the people I hate most bathe in their undeserving glory. Oh, how I wished to see them bathe in a pool of their own blood. They were the reason I was alive, but now the reason that I die, and as the burning world caves in around me, I feel my eyes blink closed for one last time. At peace. At last.

Connie Edina Gray (14)

THE KNIFE DIDN'T SLIP

The knife didn't slip. I did it. But I did it through a mask of tears. A hero would never cry while defeating a villain. He told me it wouldn't hurt; he told me all I needed to do was take the pill and it could forever end my misery. I didn't believe it wouldn't hurt, I didn't believe it would end my misery, all it would do was end my life. So, I stabbed him. I stabbed him for trying to kill me. I stabbed him for trying to make me kill myself. And I'd do it again.

Amelia Swingewood (11)

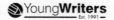

A DREAM?

A man. A shadowed face. His eyes shone blue as if reflecting a magnesium flame. His trench coat drifted along the floor hiding his legs behind a veil of silk. The man was surrounded by mystery yet felt like an open book. I could see in his muffled features a smile that appeared to smile through me as though I wasn't there. But am I? The man was both there and not like an oasis. He then reached me. His gaze looked into me and then he walked through me. I woke up, or did I fall asleep?

James Thomas

DAY OFF

I'm having a day off from being bad today to go on holiday to the Caribbean with my dog. I got her a year ago and she's called Polly. Anyway, I booked a hotel by the beach so that Polly and I can go for a walk every day. It's also going to be really awesome because there is a boat hire place and we plan to hire one for the day. Polly will love the feeling of the wind in her small labradoodle face! Hopefully, I won't miss the feeling of being bad for a week!
Yours, Venom.

Jacob Syms (13)

WHY BROTHER?

I still have not forgotten the time my whole family was wiped out from the face of the Earth by that man. Ever since, I have had a bright, blazing hatred igniting in my heart. I had revered him up until that horrific tragedy which was the day my family was killed. Furthermore, it was all for his own gain. How selfish could he get? At last, I was going to end him and finally win this war, the scene was all ready, the screams and sirens were all that was in my ears, I had won in the end.

Dennis Christopher (14)

THE WORLD OF FERAL INDIGENOUS VILLAINS

I am the villain of villains; Green Goblin! But did you know that I was never supposed to be who I am right now? I was a hero, a hero in many ways but in ways, you could never understand. The day I met Spider-Man was the day I was made a villain. All I wanted to do was show the world who I really was. I never intended on being a sinister guy who was to destroy the world like my brothers: Loki, Galactus and the Joker who were brainwashed by superheroes. Don't trust superheroes ever!

Antos Thomas (12)

OOGLERS

It was nearly time, I could feel the change in the air, my skin was as cold as ice, hairs stood to attention, a victim would be walking past any moment now. I was ready. I needed blood, not a lot, but I needed it. Ooglers had to feed every year, and it was my time. I could taste it, soft, creamy and thick. I was so ready for this. Someone will die tonight, I tried not to think about it. I see a girl, I pierced her from behind, the rush, the elation, the guilt. I live another year.

Finley Mackay (11)

THE SCHOOL FOR GOOD AND EVIL - JAPETH'S EVER AFTER

All I have ever wanted is a second chance. I want love - a happy ending, and yet my own brother voted to ditch him in the woods. Aric was the only one to love me, not even my own mother.

Every stab of my sword, every life claimed has been for him. He made me feel like I was more than evil. Aric was more than my friend - he was my brother, I loved him so much that I would give anything to see him again.

As I surrender to Death's arms, I replay the happy moments of my life...

Chloe Bromley (13)

FRIEZA'S FINAL STAND

Finally, I was about to win the ultimate prize. Wealth, fame, power, honour. The almighty Lord Frieza was about to win it all. Even with all that's happened with those abhorred Saiyan monkeys, I, the rightful emperor Frieza come out on top.

It's taken decades. Ever since that fateful day on Planet Namek, I swore to defeat him and now I prevail. I do not view myself as this tyrannical scum that I am described as. I am merely a businessman reclaiming his property.

Joe Nsengimana (13)

HAUNTED HOUSE

It was him or me. I chose me. Was I supposed to know that the house we had just broken into was the most haunted house in the area? I was the new kid in town, surely Michael should have known.

It was only supposed to be a laugh, how was I supposed to know, that only one us would escape?

That thing wanted one of us to transport its soul into. Was it wrong that I got out first? Was it wrong that I told Michael to go the wrong way when I knew what his fate would be?

Isla McCallion (11)

THE BIG BAD WOLF BACKSTORY

I never really belonged as a villain. You see my parents left me at the age of six. They left me on my own in the woods, extremely cold, no food, no shelter, no one. I had to hunt by myself. It was a hard time. I was the prey but that's why I started to hunt. I knew that to survive I had to become the predator, not the prey. I went hunting the weak, the helpless, the ones like me. Then I found the three little pigs. The three juicy, yummy pigs.

Edwin Jaimon

BOWSER'S REPENT

I had to make up for what I'd done, I needed to stop focusing on Mario and Peach and start focusing on myself and my kids. It's not my fault that Mario was always in the Bowser Kingdom stopping me from marrying Peach just because of a crush but I knew I had to give the people of Mushroom Kingdom what they deserved. So as I walked into the Mushroom Kingdom the people realised with all the goods I was carrying that I meant to harm no longer.

Benjy Harris

MY NAME IS AMÁLIA

Like any story, mine begins with my birth. I was born in Slovakia, a small town with good people as is my grandmother Lucia, who raised me. I do not know my mother or my father. I was found at the door of the church where they left me. How is it that I have a grandmother? Simply my grandmother is a nun who found me twenty years ago and gave me a home. My origin does not say who I am, just that I have a choice of who I want to be.

Liliana Janovicova (11)

AS THE WORLD CAVES IN

I have done it. I have finally found him. I found what I needed. What I needed to break. What I needed to do for the plan to finally be mine. All mine. His begging and screaming were pathetic, but that doesn't matter anymore. His work, his money, his whole wide worth will be mine. "This is your end, your demise."

Kyla Raschke (13)

NOT ON PURPOSE

It's time to come clean, people, we didn't choose this, you chose this for us. How you disliked us and the attacks to finish us were unbelievable. We will take our revenge. Our traps will be more vicious and horrible than your useless giving up attacks...

Izza Andlib (12)

![YoungWriters Est. 1991]

YOUNG WRITERS
INFORMATION

We hope you have enjoyed reading this book – and that you will continue to in the coming years.

If you're a young writer who enjoys reading and creative writing, or the parent of an enthusiastic poet or story writer, do visit our website **www.youngwriters.co.uk**. Here you will find free competitions, workshops and games, as well as recommended reads, a poetry glossary and our blog. There's lots to keep budding writers motivated to write!

If you would like to order further copies of this book, or any of our other titles, then please give us a call or order via your online account.

Young Writers
Remus House
Coltsfoot Drive
Peterborough
PE2 9BF
(01733) 890066
info@youngwriters.co.uk

Join in the conversation!
Tips, news, giveaways and much more!

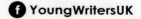 **YoungWritersUK**    **YoungWritersCW**   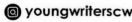 **youngwriterscw**